THE DARKLINGS

By
Jamie Timmons

For Bug; My very own Frankie,
  Without whom this book could not be. Thank you for being not only my baby sister, but my best friend.

And, for Sarah, who's bountiful laughter and second opinions made all the difference in the world.

-Haven't you ever noticed that to truly be afraid, all you really have to do is close your eyes?-

-N.J. Timmons-

I am here to share with you her story.
One I had not believed myself until it was too late.
When she came to me, she was just a child. A child
with what I had thought were mere nightmares. Some
simple cry for her parent's attention.
You don't have to believe what I am about to tell you.
God knows I didn't. But, what I have learned, I feel
necessary to pass on to others. If nothing else, to tell
the story of a simple young woman, living in what can
only be described as her own personal hell.
Feel free to dismiss it as delusion, or whatever you
will. But, what I am about to tell you is true. And,
the next time you find yourself looking into the eyes
of your child, your lover or friend…simply be
thankful that she still has them.

CHAPTER ONE:

WAITING

He stood shaking in front of the window, staring out into the street below. He took another sip of his tea, the cup clinking and chattering back onto the saucer as he put it back. A drop clung for life from his lower lip, and he carelessly wiped it away with the sleeve of his crisply starched dress shirt. Sweat poured from his brow, and tears were flooding his eyes one moment, and receding to reveal the redness the next. The bustle around them was only matched by the circus of rush hour on the streets below. Nurses and doctors, patients and family members. It all seemed a jumble of white noise and blaring irritants. It was, to say the least, unsettling. Especially considering the circumstances.

"She was doing so well…" he began. His deep voice trembling as he struggled to speak. "She was… getting better."

"You can't beat yourself up over this Dane. It's not your fault." Dr. Anderson replied. He had known Dane Welch and his family for nearly twenty years. His sister, Frankie was here in the hospital undergoing surgery. She was found in her apartment after a distressed phone call to Dane. For years she had suffered terrible delusions and hallucinations, as long as he could remember, in fact. It seemed she had taken a piece of mirror glass to her eyes in some final attempt to bore out the images she had always seen. Very sad, actually. Her therapy with him seemed to be going so well…

"She called me… she needed me, and I couldn't take enough time to help her. I just told her to calm down… that I'd be there after work." He began weeping at that point, burying his face in his hand, his back lurching with each sob. "Why didn't I just go to her when she needed me?!"

"You couldn't have known, Dane. You can't do this to yourself. I'm sure she will be fine. The surgeons here are top notch, and they are doing the best they can for Frankie. You aren't at fault for this." Dr. Anderson was doing everything he could to comfort Dane, but even he could not know whether Frankie would pull through or not. Frankie had always been a very disturbed young woman, and at this point, she had obviously been broken. He wasn't even sure if her mind could be repaired now if she did indeed survive.

"I can't understand, doc. She's gone through this since she was a kid. Nothing like this has ever happened because of it. The things she says she sees, the things she says she hears…she's never gone this far." Dane paused for a moment, still staring out the window, still holding his tea with a shaking hand. "I have a question…and, I'm not sure there's a logical answer for it." His voice shook.

"What is it, Dane?" Anderson said in his most understanding tone. But, his underlying curiosity showed through as well.

"How...." He began, but it seemed almost as though he was afraid to finish...like the answer would be more disturbing than the question itself. "How did she remove the other eye...?"

Spokane, Washington
22 years earlier

She just sat and stared at him. Dark circles around her eyes displayed a cruel lack of sleep for a child of only six. She looked tired, and she looked angry. Her expression was one of pure disdain. But, was it for him? Her parents? That's what he was there for. To find out what it was that was preventing this child from being a normal, healthy and happy six year old. Her head was pointed slightly down, and her eyes were cold and furious, looking up at him as he sat in the chair in front of her. The black circles made her look almost inhuman, close to evil. She held a teddy bear with a green bow around it's neck in her left arm, and her hair was up in pigtails, streaming down on either side of her little oval face, so worn and tired.

"Frankie, I am Dr. Anderson. I'm here to talk with you about some problems that your parents have told me about. Do you want to talk with me?"

She just stared at him, those little eyes listless and trying so desperately to stay open.

"Your mommy tells me you have some trouble staying asleep at night, can you tell me why?"

She never moved, but finally spoke. Her eyes never leaving his, the same troubling expression on her face. "They won't let me." She said in a low, scratchy tone.

"Your parents won't let you?" Anderson asked.

"No. Them." She said as she lifted her hand lazily and pointed to something behind him. When he turned, he saw nothing. Merely beige walls and a few children's finger paintings. Confused, he looked back to her. "What are you pointing at, Frankie?"

"Them. The bad things. They keep me awake at night. They won't let me sleep. They scare me so I stay awake." She said.

"What are bad things, Frankie? Are they monsters?" He asked, intrigued by her story.

"Yes. They're monsters... I think. They say things that scare me. And, they look scary. I told my mom and dad, and they didn't believe me." She said, clutching her bear now.

"And, you say they're here now?" He asked.

"Yes." She replied, pointing again at the wall behind him.

He could only think that she was having nightmares, and the fact that they kept her awake made her all the more terrified of them. She was hallucinating and seeing them now while she was awake. A delusional six year old wasn't uncommon. But, to this extent, it was unusual.

"What do they look like, Frankie? Can you tell me?"

She was silent for a moment, almost as though she was unsure of how to answer his question. "They look different all the time. Different ones." She replied quietly.

This confused him even further. Normally children put a single face on their nightmares or imaginary monsters... very puzzling indeed. "So, there's more than one? Where do they come from, Frankie?"

"They come from everywhere. I see them everywhere. Can you make them go away, please?" She sounded frightened and desperate, but her voice was so soft and tired.

"I'm sure going to try, sweetheart. But, I need you to talk more about the problems you are having. What is going on at home? Is there any trouble there?"

"No. Not really. Daddy goes to work in the morning, mommy goes to work in the morning, and Dane walks me to school. He pushes me down a lot though. He's a butt." She said as she nuzzled her bear with her chin.

Anderson laughed lightly and nodded his head. "Big brothers are like that sometimes. But, he walks with you to school, so that's a good thing. Not a lot of brothers would do that for their little sisters."

"I guess. Can you please make them go away now?" She said again. Her voice higher now, a more sincere pitch to it.

"Now? We have to work to get rid of them, sweetheart, and that takes time."

"I mean them!" She pointed to the wall behind him

again. "Make them go away!" She began shouting. Her voice frantic and riddled with fear that was impressively more profound than it had been earlier. He looked again behind him, and scanned the room trying to see what it was that frightened her so. But, he saw nothing. "It's okay, Frankie. I don't see anything. There's nothing bad here that can hurt you, sweetheart." He was trying hard to comfort the child, but she was unresponsive to his kind words. But, then without warning, she became very still. Her eyes fixed on him, the black circles around them heavy and well pronounced amidst the unusual violet colored eyes that now seemed to peer into his very being.

"Just because you don't see them Dr. Anderson, doesn't mean they aren't there."

CHAPTER 2:

VISITORS IN MY ROOM

"I've spoken to Frankie, Mrs. Welch and the only thing I can surmise is that she is a very disturbed young girl. She seems to be having hallucinations about some creatures she calls the bad things. I'm not sure what they are suppose to be, but they are quite frightening to her. She says that she sees them everywhere. And, apparently, even in my office here. Now, a concern that I have right now is, how things are at home. Is she getting enough attention and positive reinforcement from both parents?"

Mrs. Welch looked bemused and a bit concerned. Like he was saying something to her that she hadn't heard before. "We work a lot, but she gets plenty of at home time with both of us yes. You-You said something about 'bad things?' I've never heard her mention that before, Dr. I-I mean I've seen her being stern with some imaginary friends, but she never said any names or even told me about them. What did she tell you? Is my baby going to be okay? I mean, I thought she was just throwing fits, or trying to get attention." She said lightly, her hand fidgeting with the amber pendant around her neck. She was dressed like any normal parent would be. Beige wool sweater accented by a brown suede vest. She wore blue jeans and tan stiletto heels. She looked like the average American mother. Red hair, streaking with gray, oval face and fair features. She seemed nervous now, worrying about her child.

"I don't think it's an immediate concern, Mrs. Welch. Right now, I think she just needs a good night's sleep. So, what I'm going to do is prescribe some medication for her, and it should ensure that she sleeps through the night. What you'll want to do for her now is make sure that there's no added stress at home for her. She should take one of these every night before bed. And, I want a follow up appointment with her in two weeks." He said, trying to be as comforting as he could. To be honest, he never expected to see the child again. He thought she would get a good rest, and that would be the end of the delusions. He would soon find out how very wrong he was.

"Come on, sweetheart just take it. Dr. Anderson says it will make the bad dreams go away."
Frankie just batted at her mother's hand, making the pill fly across the room and bounce off of the wall.
"They aren't dreams, and I don't wanna take the stupid pill. It won't work. Nobody believes me anyway." Frankie said, hugging her pillow to her chest as she sat up in bed.
"Sweetie, it's just some bad things in your head because you can't sleep. This will help you, I promise."

"Why do you think I can't sleep then?" She turned her head slowly to ask her mother. The way she said it was nearly terrifying. Almost like a child possessed. Her mother simply looked at her for a moment. "Honey, please just do this for me. It'll make mommy feel better if you just take the pill. Please?" Mrs. Welch stepped across the room and picked up the tiny pill and held it out for Frankie. The child heaved a deep sigh and snatched the pill from her mother and swallowed it before her mother could hand her the small cup of water from the table beside her bed. Mrs. Welch sighed and ran her hand over Frankie's head gently before kissing her goodnight.

"Do you want me to leave the door open?" She asked before leaving the room.

Frankie laid down pulling the covers up to her chin and replied, "do you think it would make any difference?"

Adrienne Welch and her husband Jeffrey were hard working people living in the upper South Hill of Spokane Washington. She worked part time at a law firm doing clerical work for a stuffy overbearing boss that liked his coffee black, and his secretaries quiet. Jeffrey worked full time at a steel mill climbing the ladder to upper management, and hating every minute of it. Jeffrey worked two weekends a month, Adrienne was home with the kids most of the time. The way Frankie had been acting wasn't new. But, neither of them could explain it. She was a very sweet and loving little girl, but over the past few years, she had become quiet and distant.

Adrienne donned her nightgown and climbed into bed next to her husband. She began putting lotion on her hands and feet when her husband began to speak. "What did the quack have to say?" He snickered to her.

She sighed. "He's not a quack, Jeff. He actually gave me quite a bit of insight into what could be wrong with Frankie. He was very helpful."

He sat up in bed and closed the book he had been reading. "Yeah, yeah. What did he say?"

"He said that she isn't sleeping, and that's what's causing her to act out this way. So, he wrote her a prescription for some sleeping medication, and after two weeks, he wants to follow up with her."

"Whoa whoa wait a minute. Pills? He's got our kid popping pills?" His green eyes flared when he said it. He was furious about the idea. Their son, Dane had been on Ritalin for a year or so after a bout of hyper activity during school, it made him lethargic and tired. After they took him off of it, he was fine.

"It's essential this time, Jeff. She has to sleep, and you know as well as I do that she hasn't been. Come on, give this a chance. It might work. After all, we've tried everything else." She assured him.

"I don't like it. Not one bit." He said sternly.

"I know hun. But, it's the best shot we've got." She said. He crossed his arms over his chest and nodded. "I suppose."

Before either of them had even fallen asleep, a blood

curdling scream came from the next room. Both of them jumped out of bed and ran as fast as they could to Frankie. Upon opening her door, they found her on the floor beside her bed pulling out fistfuls of her hair. Her fingertips were tattered and bloody, and her bed was flipped upside down. She was screaming something at the top of her lungs that they could not understand. She simply kept screaming "Ne va muri niciodata!" Repeating the same phrase over and over again.

Her parents ran to her and held her until finally she became calm. Until she was simply saying "make the whispers stop... get it out of my head... make it go away." Nearly catatonic, she rocked back and forth in her mother's arms as her father rubbed her neck and shoulders gently. They just looked at each other. Something had to be done. But, what was going on? How could they fix a problem if they didn't even know what the problem was?

The next day, they were back at Dr. Anderson's office, explaining to him the episode Frankie had the night before.

"We gave her the medication you prescribed, but it didn't help. She chewed off the ends of her fingers, pulled out fistfuls of her hair and turned over her own bed. And, she was screaming in this strange language..." She said, near sobbing.

"My God..." Anderson replied. He was completely dumbfounded by this. Going to these extremes for attention simply didn't add up. "What did she say,

Mrs. Welch? Can you remember?"

Adrienne looked at him with tears flooding her eyes and running her makeup down her face. I-I think I can remember. But, it was gibberish, it made no sense at all…"

"Just repeat it to me. I may be able to make some sense of it." Anderson goaded. Jeffrey rolled his eyes and stood. "This is nonsense! Our daughter is in serious danger of bringing true harm to herself and you are talking about what it was she <u>said!?</u> What the hell is wrong with you, man?!"

"Sit down, Jeff! Just sit down! Don't you get it? We need help! And, right now, he is the best!" Adrienne yelled at him through her handkerchief. Jeffrey sat down, never saying another word. "She said Niva mari nicotine…or something like that. I can't really remember exactly what right now." She told him.

Anderson's face wore a sudden mask of shock. Color left it almost instantly and completely. "Did you hear her say…Ne va muri niciodata?" He said in almost a whisper.

"Yes!" She nearly jumped off of the chair she sat in when she said it. "What is it? What does it mean?!" Anderson simply looked at them. Puzzled and intrigued at the same time. "Has your daughter ever taken language courses? Maybe hung around with some kids that spoke a different language?" He asked, hoping there was another avenue to follow.

"N-no. She doesn't have friends outside of Dane, and she is only six…she isn't studying any other languages. Please just tell me what it means! Tell me if it means anything!" Adrienne shouted.

Anderson sighed heavily as Frankie's distraught parents waited for some answer. Anything that would ease their minds. Unfortunately, he couldn't ease their minds. For, what he was about to tell them, would bring them nothing but confusion and further worry for their precious Frankie.

"Ne va muri niciodata is Romanian..." He paused for a moment, wiping the sweat from his brow with his own kerchief before finishing. "It means, we will never die."

CHAPTER THREE:

THE BABY GROWS

"Hello, Dr. Anderson." Frankie said as she set her purse down and took her usual seat in the chair in front of him. "How have you been?"

"I've been great Frankie, thank you for asking. You're ten minutes early. We weren't suppose to meet until 11:00 AM." Anderson responded kindly.

"Yeah, my brother is planning this thing for my birthday, and I have a few things to get out of the way." She rolled her eyes and grinned, adjusting her jacket and getting more comfortable.

"Ah, yes! Happy birthday, Frankie. 18 today right?" Again she rolled her eyes. And, smiled quite broadly. "Yes." She replied. Anderson couldn't help but notice that she kept favoring her right arm. A tell of hers that he had seen several times since she was about thirteen years old.

"Can I see your arm, Frankie? Please?" He asked gently. Her smile disappeared and she suddenly couldn't look him in the eye. She focused on the table in front of her and crossed her leg over her knee, swinging it back and forth to distract herself from the unpleasant subject. "I'm fine, really."

"Frankie. We've gone over this before. Cutting yourself is just a mask to cover underlying pain. It's not even a good mask. You're scarring yourself mercilessly and for no good reason."

"It helps me think about something else." She responded. She still wouldn't look at him.

"May I please see it?" Anderson asked again.

She sighed and hesitated for a moment before removing her jacket and rolling up her sleeve. Dozens of scars revealed themselves several at a time as the sleeve receded until a fresh wound appeared. Not as deep as most others she had done, but bad enough that like the others, it needed stitches. And, like the others, she probably wouldn't get them. He held her wrist and turned her arm gently, looking over the recent and previous damage.

"Frankie…I know you have to understand the long term consequences of doing this to yourself." He said as he released her.

"Yeah, I do. But, nothing else makes me feel better. And, you know what I go through every day. We've been over this a million times." She replied.

"So, it hasn't gotten any better. You still see and hear the darklings. But, there must be other avenues, Frankie. You don't have to do this to yourself. Have you thought any more about admitting yourself into a psychiatric institution? There are some very good treatments available for visual and auditory hallucinations-" She cut him off right there. "I don't know how many times I have to say it, Doctor. They are not hallucinations. It's real. It is as real to me as the chair you are sitting in is to you. I didn't make any of it up for attention, I don't even want the attention it has brought me. I don't want these things in my life. Please, don't coddle me. Don't make me think that I'm crazy when I'm not. And, stop trying to make me think that there is something, anything in this God forsaken world that will make it all go away." She was serious, and becoming irritated with him.

"Then why do you keep showing up here every week, Frankie?" He asked, genuinely curious.

"Because Dr. Anderson, you are the only one that has ever listened to my problems. You're the only friend I've ever had, and I like seeing you." She smiled. Anderson grinned and raked his hand through his white receding hair. "Now, I've got to get going." She rolled down her sleeve, slipped on her jacket, and picked up her purse. "I have a few things I have to do. I'll see you next week." She told him as she stepped out. "Have a nice day, Frankie. And, be careful." He said as he waved behind her. After the door closed he stood up, shaking his head and scratching at his salt and pepper beard. He heaved a great sigh, wondering if she would be alright. Knowing that even after all these years, she was still trying to find someway of coping with her problems, and even her weekly therapy wasn't a complete success. She was still haunted, but by what, was still a mystery.

Dane was waiting outside in the car. A metallic mint

green Chrysler Cirrus. Brand new condition even
though it was about four years old. Dane took
impeccable care of his cars. And, he sat there listening
to the stereo and sporting the most ridiculous pair of
sunglasses she had ever seen. Of course, that was
probably the point in wearing them…to make her
laugh. Dane would have looked like a mix between
Vin Diesel and Brandon Lee if it weren't for the bright
blue highlights in his pitch black hair. He was shorter
than most men at about 5'8" and weighed nearly two
hundred pounds, thanks to a bench pressing fetish
he'd been nursing since he was sixteen. Dane was
what most referred to as a punk of sorts. But, despite
the rebellious appearance, he had a very successful full
time job in real estate that if he worked hard enough,
would turn into a very lucrative career. Most women
would consider him quite the catch…if it weren't for
those damned twirling pinwheel sunglasses. And, no
matter how hard she tried not to…of course she
laughed.

She slapped him in the back of the head on her way
around to the passenger side of the car, gingerly
opened the door and sat down. "You're such a dork."
She said matter of factually, not even looking at him
as she said it. "Yeah…but you laughed, so what does
that make you?" He replied, spinning the pinwheels
on his glasses and poking his tongue out at her. She
laughed again and he started the car…still wearing
the damn glasses.

"On to the grocery store then?" He asked as they

rounded the corner on 29th street. "Yeah." She
replied, seemingly more focused on the pedestrians
outside than she was on his question. She swallowed
hard and closed her eyes tight, pinching her pretty
face into a distorted version of what it was suppose to
be. Her hands began to shake as she closed her eyes
tighter and tighter. Dane pulled the car over as
quickly as he could and knowing what was
happening, reached into her purse and pulled out a
near empty bottle of Valium and opened it in a hurry.
"C'mon sis, take these." He spilled two pills into her
shaking hand and guided it to her mouth. She
nodded and took them, stealing a drink of his half
empty bottle of Pepsi to swallow them. "Just let those
work, okay? Let them kick in, and they'll go away.
It's gonna be fine, Frankie." He comforted her with a
gentle tone and a hand rubbing her back.
She wanted to believe that...she really did. "They
never do, Dane. They never go away. Why is this
happening to me?!" She threw her hands up to her
face and began sobbing, doing all she could to avoid
looking outside. All she would see is the twisted faces
of what were suppose to be human beings. But,
melting and distorted, charred versions of them. Skin
sloughing off in chunks and crooked black holes
where mouths would be opening up in twisted caverns
to scream at her. That was just a fraction of the
horror she would face every day. And, she grew more
frightened of it every time she saw it. But, it would be
different things each time. Sometimes it was this...

what she was seeing now. Other times much, much worse. Faces that would climb out of her walls like insects, wearing horrific expressions that only violent death could bring. Sometimes what could only be described as ghosts, gaping wounds and rotting bodies visiting her at all hours with no reason. Sometimes she would wake up to something tearing at her clothes and flesh, and she would have to explain it all away by saying she cuts herself. She never had a day of peace…and how she longed for one. But, the worst of all of them, were the darklings. Hideous wraith like creatures that moved in a series of random twitches and jerks in a manner far faster than the human body. Tall and thin with mere threads for hair stringing from their bulbous heads. Eyes round and beady, bulging from what should be sockets, but instead are hollow masses of blackness beneath their grayish leather like skin riddled with rotting patches. Frightening faces that glare their warnings, hissing whispers that tell of things no human should know… or would ever want to know. She has seen these things since she could remember. And they have sworn to her that they would never leave. Any of them. Ever. But, why? What reason could they possibly have to haunt her so? She was just a meaningless person. She was of no use to them. How could she be?

"Frankie?" Dane's voice broke her train of thought. "Frankie, are you going to be okay? Do you need to go home and lie down or something?" He sounded so concerned for her. In fact, it seemed every time he was around her during one of these 'episodes' he always worried about her. Ever since they were children. "I'll be fine, Dane. It's going away now." She lied. She wiped a lock of hair from her face and sat up straight, still trying to avoid looking out the windows. But, trying to hide it as best she could.

The grocery store was pleasantly free of more than a handful of people. It was only a bit after two P.M. and most folks were still at work now, only just beginning to worry about what was for dinner. All she had to pick up was a bag of La Choy Chow Mein Noodles, a can of chopped pineapple and four large boneless skinless chicken breast. Her brother must have Chinese in mind for her birthday dinner. Not a bad idea. She loved Chinese food almost as much as she loved Italian food. Her favorite Italian dish had to be stuffed shells and marinara sauce. Something about a medley of ricotta cheese that she just adored.

She was getting tired, and just wanted to lie down, but her brother had plans for her 18th birthday. And, she didn't want to disappoint him. It was difficult for her to believe, but she had actually procured a small studio apartment on the upper south hill, and was moving out of her brother's place in a little less than a week. She, was surprised because, she never thought she would be brave enough to venture out on her own with all the problems that she has. To be honest, she was pretty proud of herself. Terrified, and proud. In a way, she didn't want to go. But, she had to see if she could do it. Even if it didn't last, she wanted to be able to say she had at least tried.

"You about ready, sis?" Dane asked as they casually strolled through the isle containing candy and chips. This was where she wanted to be right now. Looking for chocolate. The Hershey's Symphony with toffee seemed to sing it's way into her hand and she said, "Yes. Yes I am." A smile crossing her face so wide he thought the top of her head may fall off. He laughed and they made their way to the register. Two people in front, three behind. She was beginning to feel uncomfortable being closed in that way. She took a deep breath and tried to shake it off.

 The cashier was friendly and courteous, making general conversation with Dane like most women did. Her hands began to shake again. She hated this feeling. Always when something was close by. She began to hear the whispers. Random voices hissing random words molding into sentences that made no sense to her. She began to panic. The cashier noticed it first. She asked if Frankie was okay, if she needed to sit down is all. But when Frankie looked up at her and saw the young woman smile, her pretty face was transformed into something inhuman. Her eyes became hollow and evil, her mouth twisted into some sickening smile that one might find on a demon, and her nose completely disappeared, leaving two flat hollows. Threads of blackened skin seemed to wind over it all, completing it somehow. And, of course, she would make a complete fool of herself in front of an entire grocery store by screaming bloody murder and hitting the poor woman. The whispers and hisses in her head grew louder, blaring in her mind like speakers on full volume, bass included. Trying to run was a mistake. Her head was pounding so hard that she only made it a few yards before stopping altogether. Her nose began to bleed and she could hear muddled voices behind her screaming. "Call 911! Ma'am are you okay? Frankie, come on, talk to me baby…" Then blackness. Quiet. Sleep. Thank God Dane had already paid for her candy bar…

CHAPTER FOUR:

ON MY OWN

"See you in Hell!" The voice rang out over the television. Clint Eastwood in High Plains Drifter. It was one of her favorites. She had fallen asleep on the couch watching it. And, it had, subsequently, woken her up.

Her little studio apartment was what some might have called unique. The couch sat low on the floor, as she had taken off the legs. Her bed did as well. There were lights pointed at every object in her place, from every angle. There was not a single shadow to be cast. Anywhere. That was after all, where a lot of them came from. Completely white, and boring. But, relatively safe and free of darklings. There would be some off and on, but the most severe attack she had had in recent years was at the grocery store seven years ago with Dane. She was twenty five now, and lived alone. It was by choice. She could have had her share of the male population without coercion. She just preferred to be alone.

She had been doing studies recently of the supernatural and spiritual, just to see if there was anything that could link her own situation to others. She had found several things that could have passed as related, but nothing more solid than a particular series of incidents that happened in this very state in the late sixties. That was as far as she had come so far. After a good night's rest she would continue. Her apartment was littered with open face down books, and papers strewn out like she worked for the Spokesman Review. She looked around at the chaos of it all and sighed shaking her head. Later, she thought. She turned off the television, almost reluctantly, and headed off to bed just a few yards away. She kept all the lights on. She did every night. It was hell on her power bill, but it made her feel safe. Even if it was just a false sense of security, it was some sense of security at all.

She pulled down her white blankets and sheet and grabbed a book and settled in for the night. She knew she would fall asleep reading it like she always did, and again, that was a small sense of comfort for her. She had her attention focused on something else. Over the span of years, she had somewhat trained herself to focus her attention on other things than the ones that haunt her. Simple things like books or cleaning, writing or work. It was a small thing, but it kept her from losing her mind completely. And, it wasn't long before she was asleep. With any luck, she wouldn't dream.

She thumbed through the pages of her most recent venture into the paranormal at the local library. Clacking her pencil off the table while she read, she earned herself a shush from the single librarian working today. She looked up with a small smile and nodded. The stout little woman barely acknowledged her subtle apology before going on with what she was doing. She shrugged her shoulders and took her books over to the computer to do some deeper research.

Her yahoo search under paranormal activity focused around Spokane Washington yielded many unexpected results. Her finds however were less than fortuitous, save for an article dated 1969 from the local newspaper.

The headline read:

Redimona Pruitt, Renowned Parapsychologist Found Near Dead.

The article explained that she was found in her loft, apparently the victim of a vicious assault. The assailant was never apprehended, and the case was put into the cold files after a three year investigation. Redimona had apparently told police that she was attacked by a ghost or demon...Police of course, did not believe her, as her eyes were gauged out with some household object like a spoon. And, subsequently, she was blamed her for her own misfortune, saying she had done it to herself. A gruesome tale.

A bit more research told her that Redimona had been institutionalized several years after the attack. She had a psychotic break after the police deemed the search for her attacker cold, and blamed her for the entire incident. She was held at Shady Acres Asylum for seven years before finally being released and sent back to her home. She immediately moved to the upper west side of Spokane and became a recluse. It is said that she never leaves her home, and well into her seventies now, she refuses to talk to anyone about the accident.

Her line of work before it was what Frankie was most interested in. Parapsychology was a practice with the paranormal. Namely the dead. And, Frankie needed to know if Redimona could help her to understand her visitors…maybe even get rid of them.

CHAPTER FIVE:

REDIMONA

"I'm sorry Ms. Welch, but Mrs. Pruitt doesn't see guests. She's a very solitary woman." The gentleman that answered the door was dressed in a crisp white shirt hidden under a sleeveless green sweater. His khaki pants were ironed with a crease and folded at the ankles above his black Armani shoes. His tie was tucked away beneath the sweater, and his haughty demeanor was less than pleasant. His brown hair was speckled with gray and his eyebrows were recently tweezed as evident by the red splotch between them. His hand stayed in his pocket as he leaned casually against the open door, the expression on his face was very matter of fact. She didn't even know him, and she already hated him.

"Please, it's very important that I see her. I really must talk to her." Frankie insisted.

"I'm sorry. But there's nothing I can-" He was abruptly cut off. "Let the poor girl in, Andrew. She's obviously here for a reason." The old woman caning her way toward the couch said firmly. Her white hair nearly falling over the dark glasses she wore. She was a very maternal looking figure. Mid seventies, thicker than the average female, but pleasantly plump for a woman her age. Her silk blouse had a bellow of frills spilling over the silk gray vest she wore over it. It's ties trailing behind her just above her ankles. She wore a long white skirt to accent the blouse, and what looked like nurse's shoes over a pair of thick wool stockings.

"Are you sure, ma'?" He turned to ask her.

"Of course I am. Let the poor girl in, it's freezing outside." She replied as she sat down on the sofa just parallel the door. She propped her cane against the arm of the couch and reached for the cup of tea that sat waiting for her on the coffee table. Andrew let her in and she moved quickly to the chair across from Redimona.

"Mrs. Pruitt, I need your help." Frankie began. Before she continued, the old woman began speaking to her. "I love this weather. It reminds me of my childhood here. Long Autumn days spent outside raking leaves with my father, and then jumping in them when his back was turned." She giggled like a young girl then. "I miss those days. Seems the old adage is true. Youth is truly wasted on the young." She smiled and took a sip of her tea. Her voice had an attitude to it that was bereft most women her age. Sort of alive and very aware of it…Frankie thought it was kind of nice. Redimona reached to the table and pulled out a cigarette from a silver case and lit it, inhaling the first drag deeply and slowly exhaling, letting the used smoke go up her nose.

Frankie's brow furrowed for a moment, confused at what she was seeing. "I have some questions I need to ask you." Frankie repeated.

"I know you do, dear." She took another heavy drag from her cigarette and exhaled before she spoke again. "Question is, are yours the right ones, and are you ready for the answers?" She said nonchalantly. It seemed as though she was staring right at her through the pitch glasses she wore. She could almost feel it.

"I just need to know what it is that has been happening to me since I was a child. What is wrong with me? You were a parapsychologist...can't you give me some explanation?" She asked the old woman in earnest.

"I can't if you don't tell me what it is kiddo. If you do that, we'll see what I can do for you." She said taking another drag and flicking the ashes from the cigarette directly into the ashtray beside her.

She was taken aback by that. For some reason, she just assumed the old woman had already known why she was there. Why would she assume such a thing? This woman had not even left her home since the mid seventies. She had never seen or even heard of Frankie before...

"I'm so sorry, ma'am. I got way too far ahead of myself. Let me explain." She took a deep breath, but was interrupted before she even began speaking. The old woman was laughing. Giddy as a school girl, just laughing. "No, no child. I was just kidding. You don't have to explain anything. I know why you're here." She laughed out loud as she said it. Frankie looked baffled and confused. Again she just wasn't sure what to think. How could this woman have known why she was there?

"It's alright, dear. You have no reason to worry. You said you knew I was a parapsychologist. And, that can only mean a handful of things. But, all leading to the same end. You want to know why you are being contacted...why you see things that other people don't. Why. Why. Why." She took another drag. "But are those the questions you really want to be asking?" She asked intently.

"I'm not sure what you mean, Mrs. Pruitt." Frankie replied, unsure of what to think.

She flicked another ash away and placed the cigarette in a dip in the ashtray. "Haven't you ever noticed that to truly be afraid, all you really have to do is close your eyes?" She appeared to be staring right at her. Speaking to her as though she were a long lost child, comforting and soothing, but her words were infinitely frightening to her. "People see the world around them through a veiled vision, dear. Eyes are like curtains, hiding the world outside. Yours are more like sheers. You can't see it very well, but you do see it, don't you?" She said. She seemed to understand exactly why she was there. And she never had to say a word to her about it.

Frankie replied quietly, near whispering as she said her next sentence. "I want it to go away."

Redimona chuckled lightly. "Why don't you just forget about it? Move on with your life and enjoy it, Frankie. Trust me. It's better than the alternative." She picked her cigarette back up, took a small sip of tea, and sat back. "Please," Frankie whispered, "please tell me how to make it stop."

Redimona seemed to stare through the glasses as though her eyes burned a hole through her stomach. "You are wasting your time here if you think I have an answer for you. Enjoy your life, Frankie. Just be happy you're alive." She said. "I can't! They won't let me, they won't go away!! Please help me!" She begged.

Redimona didn't even show an inkling of concern. She simply sipped her tea and held onto her cigarette, barely lit now it had been so long since she had smoked it. "Enjoy your life, child."

Frankie was losing her patience. She had taken the time to find this woman, had gone out of her way to come and see her, to maybe get some answers, maybe get rid of the problem. "You have no idea what it is I am going through. No idea." She said as she stood up to leave.

Redimona sat forward and leaned into Frankie with her next words. "You think so, child?" She removed her glasses slowly, revealing pink hollows where her eyes once were, scarred over and shrunken in. "I am the one with no eyes, young Frankie. But, you are the one that is blind." She told her. Those were the last words Redimona said to her before placing her glasses back on, leaning back again and waving her away like she was a servant.

Her hair actually flew into her face as the door was slammed behind her. "What the hell…?" She muttered angrily under her breath. But, she couldn't help but wonder what that last bit meant. While Redimona didn't have eyes, Frankie was blind? It made no sense. And, she dismissed it as just that. Nonsensical lunacy babbled by a crazy lady. Nothing she said made any sense. Simply telling her to live her life and enjoy it. And, no matter how many times she tried to tell her that the darklings would not allow her to enjoy anything, she would simply interrupt her again and babble off more nonsensical lunacy. Of course then again, wasn't she herself constantly accused of the same?

Her train of thought was suddenly interrupted by a strange whisper behind her. One all too familiar. It grew louder and louder, muddling more and more, blaring in her head until she covered her ears. "No! Not again…" She shouted. The whisper was soon followed by another, and another, overlapping into a barrage of incoherent hissing. Then she began to see them. Coming from every direction, materializing from shadows and earth, coming toward her with their jutting movement and wicked faces. Their long thin fingers reaching out as though to take her with them to hell. An eerie wind began to blow all around her, kicking up dust and debris that made it hard for her to breathe. The closer they came, the clearer she could see them. "No! Leave me alone!" She screamed at them. And, then they were there. Their heads turning themselves upside down on their necks in jerking movements that seemed surreal. She screamed out loud at them. Then they reciprocated, opening their mouths wide in a twisted and warped shape, bellowing out a sound that could only be described as a shrieking wail of noise that could have deafened anyone. "Andrew, open the door." The voice was calm. It wasn't hers. The only thing she remembered after that voice was being yanked backwards and then blackness.

"Wake up, dear." The voice was soothing as it spoke to her. "Wake up."

It was just a series of blurs when she opened her eyes. Blink. Again. She forced herself to be lucid. As her vision gradually cleared she could eventually identify her surroundings. She was back in Redimona's home. Wasn't she just kicked out? Her head was pounding. Throbbing with every beat of her heart. She could feel her pulse bursting in her temples and the pain was so immediate and so great that she thought she might faint again.

"Easy. Just easy now." The comforting voice came again. "It's all over. They're gone now."

"What the hell are these things?!" She cried out in anguish. "Please tell me! I need to know! What is going on? Why am I the only one who sees these things?" She begged for an answer. Suddenly it dawned on her. She said, 'they're gone now...' How did she know? She gave Redimona an uncertain and almost angry look. "I think you owe me some sort of explanation. Please." She said as she sat up.

Redimona sighed and sat back in the chair across

from her. She took a sip of the tea sitting beside her and swallowed hard. She then crossed her hands in her lap and eased the chair into a gentle rocking motion. "What am I to tell you, child? My explanations wouldn't satisfy what it is you want to know." She said gruffly.

"I have to know." Frankie replied, staring down at the floor. "This is all too much."

Redimona chuckled at that. She bit her lower lip gently and wiped a strand of white hair from her forehead. "Ask away, kiddo." She said almost sarcastically.

Frankie peeled her eyes from the floor and looked at Redimona sincerely. "What are they?"

"You'll have to be more specific than that, honey." Redimona replied.

Frankie wanted to throw something at her. It was a simple enough question. "What are those things that just attacked me?!" She hissed.

"Attacked?" Redimona replied, sounding almost shocked. "Oh, no honey. You weren't attacked, no. They were just saying hello. You haven't been attacked. Or you'd know it." She laughed. "They are what most refer to as shadows. A parallel to ourselves. The dark inside of us all you might say." She said matter of factually. "Most can't see them as anything more than just simple shadows. But, every once in a while…" She trailed off and took another sip of tea.

"Shadows." Frankie parroted her. She yanked up her sleeve abruptly and showed the fresh wounds, followed by the scars that covered her arm. "Shadows don't do this, Redimona!"

"Apparently, dear, yours do." She pursed her lips when she said it. Almost agitated that she was being questioned at all.

Frankie sighed heavily. "Okay, shadows. But, why? Why are they doing these things to me? Why can't other people see them?" She asked.

"There are others that can see them. But, like yourself, they just assume themselves crazy. And, sadly so does everyone else. So, they get locked away from the rest of the world and stuffed full of drugs to numb the senses. Blinding them from the world beneath the curtains. Some are blinded comfortably…Others become numb to everything." She told her, seeming to let her mind wander into another time. Her lips pursed again. She seemed almost angry now.

"Are you alright, dear?" Andrew's voice came gently from the corner of the room. He wasn't speaking to Frankie, but to his dear Redimona. "I am fine, Andrew. Another cup of tea, please love." She asked. "And for you, miss Frankie?" Andrew asked. She was almost surprised that he was being courteous to her now. "Don't seem so shocked, dear. Once he warms up, he is a very nice man." Redimona said in a low chuckle. Frankie looked back at Andrew. "Yes, I would love some tea. Thank you, Andrew." He bowed slightly and turned toward the kitchen and walked away.

"Now, where were we?" Redimona asked.

"Shadows." Frankie replied with a near whisper.

"Ah, yes. Shadows then. There are shadows, and then there are those others. I'm sure you have seen many things that you cannot explain, yes?"

"Yes...too many things."

"The ghosts are the things with the grotesque wounds and pale skin, the things that show up out of nowhere and follow you around like a lost pup are nothing to be scared of. But, there are some that are violent. Angry ghosts that died wrong. Died terrible deaths that they can't escape. Most live in the same moments over and over again. Others just want revenge for what's been done to them. And, it doesn't matter where they get it. Forget orbs and beams of light... Dust and sunshine aren't ghosts. If they want to be seen...they will be." She lit up a cigarette and took another sip of tea, just as Andrew rounded the corner holding a silver tray. He placed two cups on the table between them, with a dish of sugar and a small container of cream, with a large kettle of tea adorning the middle. He also laid out a fresh pack of Camel 99's on the table for Redimona. "Thank you, dear." She said. Andrew nodded and left. He nodded. As though she could see him. Frankie thought it was a rude thing to do...but who was she to judge? "I love when he nods..." Redimona laughed. Frankie's eyes grew wide. Redimona laughed harder. Clapping her hands together in one swift motion and leaning her head back against the chair she sat in.

"Now." Redimona said as she strangled back her laughter. You, my dear, were given a gift. Whether you want it or not, it's yours. There are very few things you could do to get rid of it. The shadows… well, they can be mean sons of bitches when they get angry. And, trying to make them leave…well, that makes them angry. And, understandably so. They have after all been here a hell of a lot longer than we have. We're just pets." She said, taking another drag from her cigarette and snuffing it out in the ashtray.

"Pets?" Frankie said, her tone questioning.

"Yes. Pets. Puppets. Little playthings to amuse them." Redimona smiled as she explained. "It's something we all live with. The world passes us by and we would go completely unnoticed were it not for the shadows. A fly on the horse's back if you will. The whole lot of us. But, there are the few of us that live with seeing them." She laughed then. "I suppose!" She finished.

"I'm not sure I understand." Frankie said, thinking aloud.

"You probably never will, and you should thank your little lucky stars for it, Frankie. When I finally understood…it was far too late." She said, frowning now. "Just leave it be, girl. You're better off just to leave it be."

She was so sincere. Her face, while void of expression, seemed to mourn, almost as if she were begging for her to just let it go. Eyes that were not even there seemed to look right through her, as though they were hiding somewhere behind the pitch glasses she wore. Trying so desperately to tell her something that her words would not allow. But, what? Why?

"I feel like there's something you're not telling me, Redimona." Frankie insisted.

Redimona just leaned her head back against the chair and sighed. She said nothing. Just lit another cigarette and rocked gently back and forth. Frankie was at an impasse. She had not gotten all the information she came for...but, she knew that Redimona Pruitt was done. She would give her nothing else. Just 'enjoy life' and 'let it go.' She knew she could do neither. Redimona had said that there were others like her. That they were locked away...

CHAPTER SIX:

ASYLUM

It seemed like such a horrible place. Walls painted with a lime green fading into a urine yellow in places, plaster visible and crumbling to the floor in handfuls. Dark warnings scrawled into them like foreboding poetry told in nightmarish haiku. Even the lobby was a hellish place. Filled with mind deserted shells of what once were functioning human beings, bumbling about in what seemed to be a mass drug induced confusion. One man sat in a corner in the fetal position wearing a bright yellow helmet, slamming his head into a wall over and over. He just kept repeating, "My name is Clyde." Frankie shivered at the cruelty of this place already.

When she finally began to make her way to the front desk, the receptionist was sitting there…filing her fingernails and chewing a piece of bright red gum. Mid thirties, bright orange hair, and neon make up that did anything but compliment her already harsh features. The tag on the front of her blue uniform read 'my name is Abbey.' Frankie hadn't even spoken to her yet, and she was already frustrated with Abbey. But, she held her tongue. Who was she to criticize how this establishment was run? She didn't work here.

She was only a few paces from the receptionist's desk when she nearly lost her footing, slipping in a puddle of urine. She choked back a mixture of disgust and anger, and proceeded. "Excuse me. I need to see a patient here…" She trailed off, noticing that Abbey was caught up in the television behind her desk, rather than paying attention to what she was saying. "Excuse me." She repeated. Abbey did not respond. She was growing angry. Slamming her hands down on the desk, she shouted. "Excuse me!!" Abbey just rolled her eyes, slowly turned her chair to face Frankie and huffed more audibly than necessary. "What?" Abbey asked in a tone less than civil. "I need to see a patient you have here." Frankie replied, trying to be as polite as possible, though she felt like ripping the woman's head off. Abbey kept chewing her gum and filing her nails, her mouth making that smacking sound every time she masticated. "Patient's name?" Abbey asked, never removing her eyes from her fingernails.

"Danika Bathory." Suddenly the smacking sound stopped and the nail file came to a halt so quickly that Frankie could swear it screeched. After a long pause, Abbey closed her mouth for a moment before replying. "Why you wanna see _her_?" Abbey asked skeptically.

"I need to ask her some questions." Frankie replied, growing increasingly more agitated.

"No one's visited her since she's been in here…" Abbey said, her tone edging on confusion. "Plus she's one of our more violent patients. You sure you're lookin' for _her?_"

"Yes, I need to speak with her now, please." Frankie said, her tone reflecting her lack of patience.

Abbey sighed heavily and stood up, taking a short few steps to the dented metal door behind her chair. She pulled out keys hanging from the superfluous ring she carried with her and jammed one into the keyhole. She looked back at Frankie with exasperation and bobbed her head in so haughty a manner that Frankie began to feel that familiar need to take her head off again. This surprised her, for she was not a violent person at all. "You coming, or did you need me to hold your hand? I got things to do you know!" Abbey snapped. Frankie fought back her urge to stab her in the eye with the closest cumbrous object, and followed.

The hall was long and narrow, trailing on for what seemed like miles with a pitch blackness at the end that didn't seem to brighten as they went further. Tortured howls and screams emanated from farther down. Louder as they moved on. Frankie closed her eyes to the blackness ahead. Too familiar with what it was now to be comfortable seeing it.

"Is there light down there?" Frankie asked.

Abbey just laughed at her, mocking her before replying. "Sounds like you should be in here with her." She chuckled.

Frankie sighed and continued on. Fortunately, there was light. They were just too far from it to have seen it right away. But at the end of the narrow hallway was a mass of locked doors and random noises from moaning floors and old rusted pipes. She could hardly believe the condition of this building. Couldn't believe that people were allowed inside it even. It was unlivable...and people were forced to live in it. Psychotic or no, no one should have to live in such miserable conditions.

Abbey halted abruptly at a door marked 3122564. An orange sign, badly frayed at the edges read, 'All visitors, caretakers and staff MUST wear protective gear at all times when entering this room.' Abbey's keys jingled in her hand as she opened the lock. Abbey was not wearing protective gear...and neither was Frankie. This hospital was a joke. Would she be hurt? Her concern was short lived, but concern nonetheless.

The door opened with a thud as Abbey yanked on the handle and a blinding light blasted Frankie's eyes when she looked inside. "Have fun." Abbey mocked as she smirked and began to walk away. "I'll assume you can find your own way out."

Frankie just glared at her as she walked away and then focused her attention on the door in front of her. The light was so bright that she had a difficult time seeing anything. Once adjusted to the blinding light she opened the door further and inched her way inside where she saw a pale haired woman, though she had difficulty accepting her age. How could this woman be sixty-six years old? She was beautiful. She sat on a mattress in the middle of the floor amid stark white walls. Nothing else was in the room. It was so well lit that not a single shadow was cast...looked vaguely familiar to her. She sat there with her knees tucked into her chest and her arms wrapped around them. Her hair was more than disheveled, it was tangled and matted to a point of being near unrecognizable as hair. Locks of it falling over her face, masking her veteran features. She rocked back and forth nervously as she slowly raised her head to peer through the white-gray locks at Frankie. She thought about turning to leave...more like running like hell...but she stood her ground and swallowed her nervous sense of fear.

"Miss Bathory?" Frankie began with an anxious tone. "My name is Frankie...I was wondering if you could answer a few questions for me?"

Danika's eyes were almost violet as she stared at Frankie through the tangles of hair that had fallen into her pale white face. It looked almost as though she wore a fine white powder. "How did you find me? Everyone should keep away. Death waits here..." She said, her expression half lunatic. Frankie thought for a moment that she had made a mistake coming here.

"I read an article in an old newspaper about you. It said you use to own the Hartwight Museum in California. That you had..." Frankie paused for a moment. "That you had a psychotic breakdown and saw things that weren't there." Frankie finished nervously. "I need to know...what it is you saw."

Danika stared at her with that same look painted on her face. Frankie was frightened for a moment that Danika might kill her…after all, it was a touchy subject for _her_, she could only imagine what it must be like for Danika Bathory. "No shadows. Shadows bring him. Shadows bring death. The devil. Death waits here. He waits for me. He waits for me to turn off the light so he can have me again. He needs to eat. No shadows." She finally said, her eyes twitching and jutting all around the room she sat in. As though she were crazed, searching for the slightest hint of what it was she spoke about. What she said made very little sense to her.

"You know about the shadows?" Frankie asked in a soft voice. Suddenly the movement stopped. Too suddenly. It was so abrupt that it made her even more uncomfortable than she already was. She almost wanted to back away.

"The shadows…" She said in a harsh whisper. "No shadows here. They come from the heart." She stood up quickly and ran around her room in a near frenzy. "You see? No shadows! Just light! They won't come from the light! It's okay here. It's okay here. It's okay here." She repeated, almost singing. "You should stay, my child. It's safe here…" Frankie backed away as she passed her. But, Danika was so quick to move back to her that she hadn't the reflexes to move away. Her face was only centimeters away from hers when she spoke. "Stay in the light." Danika whispered to her with wide eyes. "Stay in the light."

With those haunting words in mind, Frankie backed out of the room as Danika slowly made her way back to her mattress, and into the exact same position she started in. Frankie closed the heavy door and listened to the lock slide into place, feeling a sense of remorse and urgency for the insane woman now that she could not explain. Somehow, she knew. But, she was so tortured and tormented by her own mind that when she tried to warn Frankie of something impending, only gibberish came out. As she made her way back down the desolate hallway, through the screams and creaks and moans, she knew she would eventually have to come back to Danika Bathory, and somehow make some sense of what was happening.

CHAPTER SEVEN:

MEMORY

She stared out the window of her apartment at the street below. How many times had she thought about jumping? Over these many years, she had lost count. Once or twice she had even stood on her balcony ledge and tried to convince herself to let go. To make it all end…to keep them away at last. She felt so alone. Unable to make friends in fear that she would see one of them in a familiar face, and lash out at them like some maniac. All she ever wanted was someone to understand her. But, all she had was Dane. Even her parents were gone now. Her mother died in a car accident some years back, hit by a drunk driver. Both parents died that day... In a way. But, Dane, as wonderful as he was, was a big brother. He just wasn't a replacement for a friend, or a lover. She was just so alone.

A pair of ghosts in her corner were the only company she really had anymore. Twins. Little girls that seemed somehow attached to her. She paid them no mind, or at least tried not to. The more she tried to ignore them, the more she was aware of their unrelenting presence. She found herself wondering from time to time how so young a pair of children could die. She had considered asking, but thought it

would be rude. She laughed out loud then...
wondering if it were possible to be rude to a ghost.
Six years ago, she visited Danika Bathory in Shady
Acres Asylum. There hadn't been a day yet that she
had not thought of the poor woman, and the
conditions she was being forced to live in. The
darklings were still there with Frankie, always.
Unrelenting and terrifying. Every encounter meant a
new sense of insecurity, fear and loathing. And, some
visits meant new scars.
She stood sipping her tea and losing herself in her
own mind. It was the only place she had anymore
where she could find peace. No one could bother her
there...not even them. It took her nearly twenty five
years to master the skill of simply daydreaming her
life away. Though she now found it difficult not to
reminisce about her childhood. What she missed out
on because of her visitors. Tenacious and persistent as
they were. She missed all those things she never got to
do. Waking up in the morning and wondering what
was for breakfast, as opposed to staying up all night in
terror and wondering if the things she saw staring
back at her in the dark would still be there in the
morning. She wondered what it was like to play
outside. Run track. Play hopscotch. What it was like
to kiss a boy, as opposed to whether or not the boy's
face would melt into some kind of monster. How it
would feel to step into the rain and not worry about a
ghost following her. To talk to someone and not hear
the whispers of some demon trying to manipulate her

mind. Yes, she missed all those things she never got to do.

And, she wondered all the time why _she_ was the one it happened to. Why was she the one with this absurd 'gift.' She didn't want it. She hated every minute of it.

Spokane Washington,
24 years earlier.

"Frankie sweetie, I just need you to help me here. What is it you are hearing right now?" Anderson asked in his most gentle tone.

"I don't wanna talk about it!" She screamed at the top of her lungs. Her little hands were clenched over her ears so tight that he thought her little eardrums might burst from the pressure. She was pacing around the room like some kind of terrified caged mouse.

"Frankie, please sit down, honey. We need to get through this if we're going to make it all stop. You need to talk to me, please." Dr. Anderson said.

Suddenly she stopped dead in her tracks, removing her hands from her ears slowly. Her little eyes wide and bugging now. Like she was terrified and frozen. She stood in silence staring off into nothingness.

"Frankie?" Dr. Anderson said with concern. Frankie did not respond. She simply stood there, stiff as a board, those pretty little eyes wide with terror.

Anderson reached forward and placed a hand on her arm to comfort her, or try to get some sort of response from the catatonic child. But, as soon as his finger tips touched her, he was thrown back by some unseen force. It was like a hand, clammy and cold and rickety, tossing him backward over his chair with the force of a championship prize fighter. He slammed into the curio cabinet on the other side of the room and shielded himself from the rain of glass that showered over him when it shattered. It took him a moment to gain his bearings, but when he finally looked back at Frankie, she still stood there. Her nose and eyes were dripping with blood, but she remained perfectly still. What the hell just happened? Was she seriously being haunted by these things? Or was her mind so convinced of it that when she told him these stories, he was beginning to suffer the delusion as well?

He stood slowly and started to walk toward her, the sound of glass crunching beneath his feet. He approached her cautiously and eased his hand in again to touch the poor child's shoulder. This time he was able. As soon as his hand made contact, the child collapsed and began to sob. Tears and blood soaked her cheeks as Anderson lowered her to his lap and began to wipe her face with a kerchief.

"It's alright, kiddo. It's all over now. It's all going to be okay." He said, doing all he could to comfort the child, while he himself remained frightened and confused. He looked at his wrist…the faint beginnings of bruises were already forming there. Imprints of alien like fingers the like of which he had only seen on the thin and elderly population. He looked down at Frankie, the poor child riddled with fear, shaking like a leaf and sobbing. When the sobbing ceased so suddenly, Dr. Anderson showed concern, fearful that it would happen again. Instead, she just looked up at him, her brown eyes flooding with an ink like blackness. She spoke then, but it wasn't in her voice. Not the voice of a child. But, more like that of some demon.

"Ne va muri niciodata!!!"

 Reality slapped her in the face with a knock at the door, nearly dropping her cup of tea, she tried to catch her breath. "Who is it?" She shouted. No answer. She hated that. It was probably Mormons again, trying to spread the word of God or maybe the girl scouts peddling cookies and pamphlets which she had refused so many times she lost count. "Hello? Who's there?!" She shouted again. Finally she gave up her perch and went to the door. When she flung it open, no one was there. She scanned the hallway up and down, but not a whisper of any presence was there. She sighed and slammed the door. She needed some clearer answers. Someone who would really know what was happening to her. She had to go back to see Redimona. She was choiceless now.

CHAPTER EIGHT:

LOST SOURCE

The driveway was packed with city personnel vehicles. Ambulance, police, coroner. This couldn't be happening. What the hell was going on? She ripped through the line of yellow tape barricading any unwanted visitors outside and shoved her way through the sea of blue suits and ties. Gold badges and tiny flip notebooks with matching pens flooded the once peaceful home of Redimona Pruitt. But, so far, she wasn't to be found.

Andrew stood sobbing in the corner of the dining room. Frankie seemed to go unnoticed. She ran as quickly as she could to him and grabbed his arm, startling him. He looked at her almost damningly. "Andrew, what's going on? Where is Redimona?" Frankie asked near panic.

"She's…" Andrew trailed off.

"Answer me, Andrew. Please."

He looked at her with red puffy eyes, like a wounded dog with no owner to crawl back to. "Andrew Please!" She grabbed his shoulders and shook him violently. He sobbed harder then.

"She's…gone. She's gone. My Redi is gone!" He choked out between sobs.

"Andrew…" Frankie whispered. "What happened to

her?"

He looked at her in fear. Almost unknowing of what he should say, or how he should say it. "She...said too much. She wanted to call you. To...tell you what to do." Andrew spoke softly.

"Tell me what, Andrew? Talk to me please." Frankie begged.

"She couldn't take it anymore." He said. "Living with those things...all the time. She couldn't take it anymore." He began to sob uncontrollably. "My sweet Redi. I love you." It was the last time she would hear him speak. Andrew was a broken man now without his sweet Redimona. All he would do now is cry. She was his life. Frankie knew that from the moment she met Andrew. What would become of him now?

"Excuse me, ma'am. You shouldn't be here." A deep voice boomed behind her. When she turned, a large man in a black police uniform stood there with his hand gently on her elbow, kindly urging her to leave.

"I...I knew her. She was my friend." Frankie said.

"Then you must be Frankie Welch?" The officer asked.

"...Yes. I am. Why do you ask?" Frankie replied, confused.

"I'm officer Moore. Please come with me, Miss Welch. We have to talk." The officer said as he guided her from Andrew to the porch outside.

"What's going on, what happened to her?" She insisted.

The officer took his hand from her elbow and looked at her for a moment. "How well did you know Redimona Pruitt, Miss Welch?" He asked her.

"Not very. We only met once about six years ago. We talked for a few hours about…some common interests and I left." She told him hesitantly.

He squinted and slung a gloved finger across the bridge of his nose before speaking. "She left this." He said, pulling a crisp, pearl colored envelope from his jacket pocket. "It's addressed to you." He said before handing it to her.

Frankie was confused. "Shouldn't you keep this for evidence or something? Try to figure out what happened to her?" She asked.

He looked at her, almost with a mixed expression of sadness and disgust. "We don't need an investigation, Miss Welch." He said quietly, looking now at his feet. He looked back up at her, squinting at the mid morning sun. "Her nephew found her this morning in the bathtub. She had chewed through her own wrists and bled to death last night." He gave her a pitiful look and squeezed her shoulder. "I'm sorry. But, for whatever reason you came, it's best to just go back home until we're done here. Then, in a few days, come back and see Andrew…maybe make sure he's alright." He paused for a moment then. "She was pretty much all the guy had left in the world." The officer nodded and walked away.

Frankie clutched the envelope to her chest and stood there with a horrified expression painted on her face.

Redimona? Killing herself? There had to be some other explanation. Redimona hardly seemed the type to commit suicide. She was a very proud, cheeky and imperious woman... Chewing open her wrists? She could hardly believe it. No. She wouldn't believe it. It simply wouldn't have happened. But...how did it happen then? Who or what killed Redimona Pruitt? Certainly not Andrew. He simply loved and adored her too much to bring harm to her. "Oh, and Miss Welch?" The officer turned back to her after having taken only a few short steps. He removed his cap and scratched his head before continuing. "Miss Pruitt had no eyes..." He began. He heaved a confused sigh. "And, Andrew said he didn't write the letter...we even compared handwriting samples just to be sure." He stopped and scratched his head again. "She had no eyes, Miss Welch...how did she write the letter...?" It wasn't a question he expected any answer to. He handed her a card and sighed heavily. "Please, call me if you need anything." He just placed his cap back on his balding head and walked away, his expression one of deep pondering. Frankie looked down at the envelope clutched in her hands and furrowed her brow. Something evil was happening here. What would she do now?

CHAPTER NINE:

TWO LITTLE GIRLS

She sat there on the edge of her mattress, staring down at the wrinkles in the comforter now adorning the floor since she woke up. She had been blankly staring like that for at least an hour now. She hadn't even made coffee. Was all of this really happening? Was Redimona Pruitt really dead? Was it because of her somehow? She didn't want to think about it...but at the same time, she couldn't stop. She hadn't even read the letter that Redimona left for her. She wasn't even sure she ever would.

A pair of young twins stood staring at her from the far corner of her apartment. They had been there off and on for upwards of three months. Just staring at her. The more she ignored them, the more tenacious they became with their presence. Frankie was yet unsure of how to even acknowledge them. They were the first ghosts to ever have hung around for more than a few startling seconds. What startled her more than that, was that she was becoming use to them being there. But, they just stared at her. Two young girls, no more than eight or nine years old with light brown hair and greenish blue eyes. They wore a light blue dress with a bow around the waist, and a blue ribbon around their loose hanging hair. Little black slippers on their tiny feet with frilly socks to accent the dress. Both had their hands folded neatly in front of them and a look of pure question on their powder white little faces.

Frankie sighed heavily and rubbed her hands down her face. "Okay. I give up. What do you want? Why are you here?" She said aloud, looking to the far corner where the girls stood staring at her. They merely cocked their heads to the side slowly as though they weren't quite sure if she spoke to them or not. So, she said it again. "What do you want from me?" She repeated. They did nothing. Their heads stayed cocked to the side, and they remained there, staring silently at her. She growled out loud at the frustrating quiet and stood abruptly making a beeline for her coffee pot. All she had to do was flip a switch and the smell of fresh brewing coffee filled her nostrils. She loved that smell. She looked again at the tiny visitors standing in her corner and thought for a moment. It shouldn't be too hard, she thought, to get information on twin deaths. Her computer was, after all, her best friend in the world. She rolled her eyes then, sad to be admitting that to herself.

After a few minutes had passed, she poured herself a cup of coffee, added her usual Mocha Mix and made her way to her laptop, sitting down on a pillow and taking a sip before turning it on. Immediately she double clicked the internet icon and waited for the page to load. She typed 'twin deaths' in her search engine and was astounded at the mass of results she found there. 12,144,349 results found for 'twin deaths.' She wanted to throw it across the room. She sighed heavily and looked across the room to her waiting, and uninvited guests. Their heads still cocked to the side, they stood there, just staring at her. She took another sip of coffee. "Fine." She said. And returned her attention to her laptop screen.

One by one she checked the results of her search. Finding nothing to match the girls haunting her apartment. Six cups of coffee, two bathroom breaks, and 312 results later, she found something.

Search for missing girls called off. Police have no new leads.

'The search for missing twins Heather and Marianne Ingram, age 8, is called off after sixty days of extensive searching. Spokane police say 'they are baffled and exhausted, but if the girls haven't been found by now, we're afraid they never will be.' The girls are presumed dead, and a memorial service will be held Monday, March 12, 1998. Police encourage anyone with information about the missing girls to still come forward."

Frankie looked up and saw the two girls still standing there. But, they had a new look on their faces now. Almost a blank sense of urgency. As though her silent friends were encouraging her to keep going. Keep searching.

She typed the names Heather and Marianne Ingram into her search engine. Far fewer results. But, exactly the ones she was looking for. The first result yielded

the information she needed. There was even a picture
of the girls there, wearing the same blue dresses, the
same hair, even the same little shoes. "There you are."
She whispered.
Missing girls assumed dead.
The search continues for twins Marianne and Heather
Ingram, missing since Tuesday night. Parents Heather
and Brendan Ingram say, 'we had tucked the girls in
after their bath at nine o' clock, when we went back to
check on them at eleven, they were gone.' Police say
the windows in the girls' room were painted closed,
and no intruders could have come into the house
without Heather and Brendan's knowledge. Parents
say that nothing in the girls' room was out of the
ordinary, and there is no explanation for their
disappearance. Heather and Brendan Ingram are still
being held for questioning now seven days into the
search.
  Frankie was confounded. Had the parents killed the
girls? She looked again to the corner across the room.
But, this time the girls weren't still. It was like a tape
being played in reverse, but skipping frames. The
movements were quick and jerky. And, the girls
seemed to be frightened now. Frankie was becoming
frightened as well. But, this time she was scared of
what it was she was seeing. It went on for a few
seconds like that, like they were struggling in reverse
to free themselves of something, until the girls became
suddenly frozen and vanished into thin air. Like puffs
of smoke they were gone. And, as they vanished she

could hear tiny voices, frightened and desperate. "It's coming for you!" Frankie was frozen.

She took in a deep breath and looked back to her computer screen at the image there of the two young girls. They were haunting her for a reason. And, if she wanted to get rid of them, she had to find out what it was. She remembered the card that officer Moore had given her the day before. Rummaging through her purse, she found it among a rubble of old receipts and Starbucks gift cards. She stared at it for a moment, contemplating on whether or not she should really do what she was thinking of doing.

A moment later, she picked up her phone and dialed the number. It rang only twice before the familiar voice answered. "Hello, this is Moore." Frankie paused, unsure of what she should say. "Hello?"

"Yes, officer Moore? This is Frankie Welch. We spoke yesterday at Redimona Pruitt's house." She finally said.

"Yes, I remember. How can I help you Miss Welch?" He asked in a bland tone.

"Well..." She paused for a moment. "I was hoping to get some information on two missing girls. I'm not even sure if you're able to do that or not, but...it's really been bothering me." She forced out.

There was a brief silence over the phone. "Okay... what girls?" He asked, his tone slightly hinting suspicion.

"Their names are Heather and Marianne Ingram. They went missing in 1998."

Another long pause. "Ingram..." He repeated. "Yes, I remember them. They were never found. Not hide nor hair of them. They just disappeared one night." He said, his voice reminiscent. "I actually worked that case. You said it was bothering you? How is that? Did you know them?" He asked.

"No." Frankie said. "But, it bothers me. I can't explain it, but I really need to get to the bottom of it. Can you help me?" She said in earnest.

"Well, Miss Welch, the case is cold. I can give you all the information I have, but as far as anything goes, you won't likely get any farther on it than I did. No offense." He said with a chuckle.

"None taken."

"Why don't you come by the precinct, and we'll have a talk about it. It's a lot to go over on the phone. I have a break coming in about an hour, usually never take them, but in this case I'll make an exception." He said lightheartedly.

"Thank you, Mr. Moore. I'll be there." Frankie said before exchanging goodbyes and hanging up the phone. What the hell was she doing? She asked herself as she placed the card back in her purse and headed out the door, but not before taking one last look at the now empty corner on the far side of her apartment.

"I've seen these children before, Mr. Moore. But, I

can't explain it to you in a way that you would understand, or even believe me." Frankie said, her tone near exasperation.

"Why can't you explain it to me? I'm here. I'm listening." He replied. His arms crossed over his chest. His expression was one of questioning and concern.

She tried to think of some way to tell him. But, if he was like everyone else, he would just call her crazy and shoo her away like some irritating fly. "Can I just please get the information on those girls? It's really important to me. There's something I have to figure out."

He sighed heavily and tipped his chair back, his arms still crossed. "I think I deserve some sort of explanation for all of this Miss Welch. I really do. And, until I get something to go on with all of this, I feel no obligation to help you by giving you information on a dead cold case." He said matter of factually. "Now, you said you've seen Heather and Marianne Ingram before. Where did you see them?"

Frankie hesitated. Unsure of what to say...or even how to say it. She knew what he would think of her. But, she wouldn't get the information she needed without telling him everything. "Have you ever worked with psychics in your department, Mr. Moore?" She began.

Moore's face twitched with question. He sat his chair down on all four legs and leaned forward. "A few off and on, why?"

"Well… I have something of a… gift." She said, her voice cracking and filled with nervousness. She swallowed hard and looked at him.

"So, you're a psychic." He said.

"…Not quite. I um… I see things." She said. Her hands were beginning to shake now.

Moore cocked an eyebrow and looked at her, focusing mainly on her body language and how nervous and agitated she was becoming about the subject. "You see things like what?" He asked, trying to ease the tension building in her. Trying to get her to talk about what it was she was so desperately trying to get off her chest.

She lowered her head and tried to focus on keeping her hands still. "It's hard to explain. I just see things that other people can't see. And, I get a lot of grief about it." She said.

"Okay. So, you see things. Like what? Ghosts?" He asked gently.

She snapped her head up and looked at him with wide eyes. "That's some of it. But, yes. And, I have seen those girls in my apartment. The ghosts of those girls. Now, could you please just give me the information I need without humiliating me any more? Please?" She asked.

Moore looked at her with an expression mixing sympathy and earnest. He didn't respond right away, but sat there, just looking at her like that. He wasn't sure whether he should believe her, or follow his first instinct of locking her up in Shady Acres with the rest of the crack ups in this damned city. He decided to go undecided, but to help her. She wanted information on a cold case, she could have it. It had haunted him for years, and he was done with it. Hell, she could take the whole damn file for all he cared. He stood without saying anything and left the small office they sat in. Not even a look to tell her what it was he was going to do next. He just got up and left.

 She scanned the room around her. Just what you would expect from a run down precinct office. Brown fading paint, a few pictures of family dusted over from years of build up, an old air conditioner sitting precariously in an open window, blue plastic stringers flying from it as though desperate to escape. The ceiling drooped in one corner from what looked like had been a leak some years back, with a brown orange stain adorning it with just the right amount of color to lend stability to her theory. The window was cracked just above the bottom of the frame in a crescent shape, like the chair he sat in had been tipped back just a bit far at one time. The computer sitting on his desk was so out of date she could have used it as a child, and a small hand held television sat askew on the far corner with a bent antennae and a broken power knob. His coffee cup had a handle that had been glued back on, and stains on the inside from years and years of use, it read 'Super Cop.' Kind of cute, she thought. Something a child would give to their father or uncle.

 The door kicked open after a few moments, startling

her. Moore started in the room with a box in his arms and plopped it down on the desk in front of her. "Here it is. All the case files on Heather and Marianne Ingram." He said, winded. He stood there with a hand leaning on the corner of the desk, trying to catch his breath. "Take it." He finished.

Frankie stood and looked at the box before her. Then looked at officer Moore. "I don't know how to thank you for this. It means so much to me." She said, placing a hand on his shoulder. He simply nodded his head and moved to the chair across the desk and sat down.

"You'll let me know if you need anything." He said. It wasn't a request. It seemed to be a demand. Was he so concerned?

"I will. And, thank you again." She said before picking up the box and looking at Moore for a moment. "Why do you believe me when no one else does, officer Moore?" She had to ask.

He looked at her, his hands behind his head and his chair tipped back on two legs again. "I never said I did." He began. "But, I wanted an explanation and you gave me one."

She took a deep breath inward and sighed, lowering her eyes to the box in her arms. "Thank you, officer Moore." She repeated as she walked out of his office.

CHAPTER TEN:

MOURNING

The case files lead her to where the girls' parents had been staying. An old retirement home off of nine mile called Sundance Meadows. She was nervous. Unsure if she wanted to talk to them or not. But, she needed information. Information she wouldn't get out of that little box with all the papers in it.

It was a very lax environment. It was a place that seemed to offer a good amount of freedom to the elderly. Clean, serene and comfortable. But, with enough nurses and aides roaming about to offer a sense of security that most people that come to a place like this would need.

The nurse's desk at the front of the main building was a far cry from the one at Shady Acres Asylum. Very neat, clean. And polite.

"Hello, I am Frankie Welch. I am looking for Heather and Brendan Ingram. Are they here?" She asked lightly.

The nurse looked at her and smiled. "Yes, they are. It's so unusual that they have visitors. Normally they just sit here alone, looking out the windows and holding hands. They are a sweet old couple, but I think that they are really lonely. It's nice of you to come and see them." She said as she took Frankie's name down on a visitor's list, came out from behind the desk and motioned to walk with her. As she did, she noticed the corridors well lit, art lining the walls and a variety of plants here and there. It was a pleasant scene. Not at all like she would picture a nursing home to be. "They are pretty quiet normally, but I think maybe they would warm up to you if you just give them some time to get use to you. We try to encourage socializing here, but these two keep pretty much to themselves. They aren't disruptive or anything, just quiet. They lost their kids a long time ago, and I don't think they ever really got over it. Twin girls I think." The chipper nurse said as she walked in front of Frankie. "It's actually really sad how a loss like that can affect you for so long." She continued. "You have a visitor! This is Frankie. She's a very nice lady." She said as she opened a door. Inside sat two well aged people, maybe mid to late sixties, sitting in front of a window, holding hands. "I'll leave you folks to get to know each other." The nurse said as she walked away, leaving the door open. Frankie stepped inside, unsure of how to even begin. She took a seat next to Mrs. Ingram and looked quietly for a moment at the couple. Their eyes never moved. Staring blankly out the window in front of them as though they were the only two people on earth. Never speaking. Unmoving. It was almost eerie seeing it.

"My name is Frankie." She began in a quiet tone. Almost afraid she would disturb them. They did not answer. Only stared out the window. Fixated on it. "I was hoping maybe you could answer some questions for me…" she hesitated a moment, "About your daughters."

Like a shot their heads turned at once, in strange swift movement as though their heads were trying to work themselves off their shoulders. wide eyes tearing through her like glass. Their expressions ones of concentrated shock, both the same, both pointed at her. Their hands still locked together as if they were glued that way. It was unnatural movement. Unnatural expression. And it terrified her. She closed her eyes against it tight and told herself it wasn't real. Even though she knew it was. A way to delude herself into a small amount of comfort perhaps. When she opened them again, they sat, as they had before, just staring out the window. Blankly. Without expression. As though she had not said a word to them.

"Mrs. Ingram?" Frankie said in a low tone.

"They are gone." Mr. Ingram said briskly. Frankie was set aback for a moment. Unsure that he had spoken. "They were taken from us long ago." Mrs. Ingram put in. Neither of them turned their eyes from the window. They simply stared, even as they spoke. As though they weren't even there. "Our home…" Mrs. Ingram trailed off then, seeming as though her mind had wandered and lost itself in her own thoughts. Mr. Ingram continued for her then. "It was late. All we did was go to check on them like we did every night. Every night. Just to make sure they were okay." He recited it like a story. Something he had told a million times. Maybe to himself to ease his suffering of the loss. "They were gone. Our girls. Just gone. As if they hadn't been there at all." She could see the hurt show in his eyes as he said it. Though his eyes never left the window. Mrs. Ingram shuttered then, clasping her husband's hand tighter, just staring. Frankie wondered only for a moment what it was they were looking at. When she looked herself she saw only trees and gardens. She wondered if they saw the same. "That house…" Mrs. Ingram began softly. "Our home… Is evil." Frankie just looked at them. Their loss was great. So great she couldn't even imagine what they must have gone through. Or what they must still go through to this day. Did they murder their own children? Likely not. And she had to find out what happened to Heather and Marianne Ingram. Not just for their parents… But for the girls themselves.

CHAPTER ELEVEN:

DARK FLOORS

Boarded up windows. Peeling forest green paint. Short picket fence leaning and bowing on one end, worn down from time and element. A small pond that had gone dryer than a bone with neglected toys and inflatable animals laying where water use to be. A broken down swing set barely stood in the back yard on a dusty patch of earth adorned with weeds and dead flowers. Trees with hand like branches reached down toward it like ghostly fingers to snatch up whoever was brave enough to come near. Graffiti littered the entire home on the outside, even the condemned sign clinging to it's hook for dear life in the front yard had some unreadable nonsense scrawled on it in a festive green and red. The doors hung open, barely clinging to the hinges.

She shouldn't be here. She knew it. She could feel it. But, she had to. It was the only way she was going to find anything. They wouldn't haunt her if they didn't need her for something. Right? She questioned herself then. And not for the first time. Was anything she saw or heard real? Was she crazy? No. She shook her head then. Too much added up. This was not in her mind. The steps groaned and cracked as she made her way to the back porch and peeked through the open door. A kitchen, worn down by years of abandon, smelled like dust and mold. Pots and pans still hung from a rack above a small island across from a stove with blackened patches and rust stained burners. When she stepped inside she was taken aback by the strong odor of mildew and almost reconsidered venturing further. It took her a moment to regain her bearings. She blinked wide and hard for a moment, pinched her nose and shuffled on.

It could only have been described as a lost place. Trapped somewhere in time. It was as if it had simply been abandoned, it's inhabitants vanishing. Frankie felt uncertainty, and a creeping sense of unease as she stepped through the kitchen.

Used china sat on the table, clothed in a layer of dust so thick the bugs even avoided it. A glass pitcher with what at one time must have been liquid sat in a greenish yellow ring to the left of a gravy boat, cracked and worn with time. A sterling serving platter with holes rusted through the bottom lay on the floor next to a cracked table leg that had been repaired in the good ol' honey-do fashion that it seemed all married men used. Duct tape and screws. She giggled in her throat then, remembering all the honey-do fix it's that her father had performed, cutting corners to save time. She even remembered when he tried painting the duct tape to match the table. Didn't work out so well if she recalled correctly. Mom had a fit.

The dining room just off the kitchen displayed a china hutch, glass shattered and more graffiti reading

"Rico" adorning the front. Charming, she thought sarcastically to herself. Pin striped wallpaper tattered the entire room, like claws had ripped through it in protest of the pattern chosen. Off the dining room was an office. Children's toys strewn about as though they had just been here, were it not for the grime, dust and mold. A Tudor style desk sat to the far right, papers decorating the top and floor about as though someone were having a tantrum, or a party at some point.

The dining room led to the living area through a T shaped arch, trinkets and nick knacks neatly in their places on the adjacent shelves, blanketed in dust. It was an eerie sight to behold. Ghostly. Furniture had been overturned, holes chewed into most of it by rats. Cut up by transients and thugs.

Everything was in it's place... and somehow wasn't. Light seeped through cracks in the walls like a silver halo, threading over the room in beams of veiled dust, climbing up walls and over ceilings like the fingers of some ghastly creature.

The stairs creaked and groaned beneath her feet, making her think twice about climbing them further. Holes adorned the walls where pictures had once hung neatly in place. There was only one room when she reached the top, oddly free of furniture of any kind. But, the room looked like it belonged at one point to children. The walls were painted in an off tone blue, streaming with pink painted ribbons and stars on the ceiling. The closet door hung open, barely hanging by it's hinges, with nothing inside but blackness.

Unsure if she should venture further, she cautiously stepped forward to peer inside. Her heart raced inside her chest, knowing too well what the darkness brought. And, what it brought was never pleasant.

Nothing. Empty and bleak. A simple, ordinary child's closet. Nothing remarkable to speak of... Save for the pitch blackness inside. With a shudder, she stepped out and closed the door. Awkwardly, her attention now focused on the wood floor beneath her. The planks, molded and rotting away, separating to reveal an uncomfortable darkness beneath. Loose and wobbly, the boards groaned and sank beneath her feet as she walked over them, peering between them to reveal a mysterious blue. She halted suddenly at the familiar shade and cringed inwardly. It couldn't be.

Stepping adjacent she ripped the remnants of lace curtains, tattered and torn, from the small rectangular window, allowing enough light to peer into the room and illuminate the floor. She needed only a moment to let her eyes adjust to what it was she was looking at. Before even realizing she had lost the will to stand, her knees hit the rotting floor with a loud thud. She just sat there now trying not to cry.

Anger, fierce and wild welled up inside of her with an intensity matched only by the urge to run and never look back. But, she couldn't do that. With a scream loud enough to wake the dead, she began to pound relentlessly on the rotting wood until it gave beneath her fists. Cracking and groaning, splintering and buckling, revealing it's long hidden secrets.

The hole was big enough now for a small person to fit into. Tears soaked her face and her hands stung and bled. Hair fallen from it's catchings now clung to her face as she sobbed. All she could do was cry as she stared down at the blackened, shriveled bodies of two twin girls. Their faces twisted with fear, one sister's hand clasped the others. They wore a light blue dress with a bow around the waist, and a blue ribbon around their loose hanging hair. Little black slippers on their tiny feet with frilly socks to accent the dress. Heather and Marianne Ingram... Found at last. She wanted to die then. Leaning back, she put her head against the wall and just sat there.

CHAPTER TWELVE:

MOORE'S THE PITY

She sat staring out at nothing from the back of an ambulance, her hands stinging and wrapped with gauze. Her face was filthy, streaked with dirt and tears, hair still clinging to it from her earlier fit. In front of her stood Moore. She wasn't sure yet if this was good, or bad. "I remember this place," he began as he stared up at the derelict house, his hands on his hips, "We searched every damn inch of it... Top to bottom, front to back..." he trailed off as though he were reliving the search itself. "Not once... Not once did we even consider those poor girls were buried in the floors..." He ran his hand over his face and looked at Frankie. "You OK, kid?"

She wasn't positive how to answer. She wasn't OK. She would survive. But, she wasn't OK. "I'm fine, thank you..." It wasn't true, but it would have to settle. She stared down the street where a crowd had gathered a few moments earlier. It astounded her that wherever there was tragedy, there were eyes eager to see it. Humanity was a loss in it's entirety, she thought. Did she mean it? At this point she couldn't tell.

She turned her gaze to the trees in the distance and couldn't help but wonder how beautiful they must look at night. Night... Something she hadn't seen since she was a child. The skyline glowed a bright yellow now, and her concern began to rise like a knot lodging in her stomach. It would be dark soon. She needed to get home. "Officer Moore," she began. He stared intently at the second floor window, his face a mask of dread and self-loathing. "Call me Bert," he replied, his eyes staying fixed where they were.

"I need to get home soon," she said quietly, turning her head upward to try and see what had his attention. "How many times," he began softly, "how many times did I just *walk* right over 'em? Never in a million years would I have known... But, you... you knew." He seemed almost frustrated with her. Was it her he grew angry with or himself? Perhaps the question was best left for another time.

"You couldn't have known..." she tried to console him, touching his arm.

"Yeah..." he replied quietly as he choked back his emotion. "So it was the damn parents, after all. And, now they're wasting away in an old folks nut hut. Couldn't arrest or prosecute if we tried. Fantastic. Those girls, they died that horribly... And, they go without justice even now," he said as he stared up.

Was there really any way at all to explain that the parents were indeed innocent? Would he believe her if she tried? Just then a coroner's van backed onto the lawn. She hadn't even noticed they arrived. She watched intently as two gentlemen entered the home with body bags draped over their arms like they were jackets. So casual were they that Frankie almost lost sight of what they were there to do.

Pink and purple hues began to decorate the horizon now. It had been so long since she had seen the dusk that she had forgotten just how beautiful it was. Especially this time of year. With all she had missed in her life, there were times she couldn't help but wonder if she was being punished somehow for some dastardly act she was unaware of committing. Perhaps in a different life. If indeed there was such a thing.

"Christ, I can't believe this..." Bert said as he worried his bald spot with his bare hand. Frankie almost wanted a comical squeak to erupt when he did it. But, alas... "Damn nightmare is what this is... a Goddamn nightmare..." he finished. If only he knew, she thought. And, she hoped it wasn't out loud.

More faces appeared in the growing crowd. It was beginning to feel like a show. These poor little girls were becoming an attraction. It embarrassed and disgusted her at the same time... Moore seemed use to it. Part of his job, she thought. But, how could someone get use to something like that? All those people, turning despair and hurt, tragedy and loss, into entertainment? They gawked on as though it were fun. She wondered then if any of the older faces she saw knew the girls... If any of them even understood what was happening here... She couldn't imagine any human being would still be standing there watching like it was a television crime drama if they knew... She wanted to have more faith in the human race than that.

It didn't take long for the coroners to emerge from the house carrying the same bags. A man at each end holding separate corners as normal procedure would indicate, and yet the bags looked as empty as when they went inside. It would have taken a skilled eye to be aware that there was anything inside them at all. Frankie cringed inwardly and looked away.

"Don't worry, Miss Welch," Bert began as he finally freed his gaze from the window to match hers, "we're gonna get you home." He looked at her with a mixture of question and fear. There was something he wanted to ask her, and she could see it, almost as clearly as she could see his discomfort. "How?" He finally spit it out after staring at her for several moments. She merely raised an eyebrow to his query. "How did you know... where to look," he clarified. She matched his gaze with a blank expression and thought about how to answer. To hell with it, she thought. Just be outright honest.

"It was the darkest place in the house."

CHAPTER FOURTEEN:

A MOTHER'S LOVE IS A MOTHER'S LOVE

She stared at her light switch without blinking, waiting for sleep to come. After the day she had she wondered if sleep would come at all. How many times had she thought about turning it off? About turning them all off...? Wondering if maybe it would help. If maybe it was all in her head and facing the dark would just make it all stop. It seemed so logical. But, it had been tried before...

Spokane Washington,
20 years earlier

"Please, mom. Don't let them put me in there. It's dark in there. That's when they come, is in the dark." Frankie pleaded with her mother who simply stood there, holding her hand. "Frankie honey, that's why we need to do it. So you'll see sweetie, there's nothing in the dark to be afraid of. It's all bad dreams baby, you'll see."

Frankie turned her attention to the nurses blacking the windows of a very small room recently used for storage... Dr. Anderson had it cleaned out strictly for this experiment. Convinced that if she were forced to face her greatest fear, she would no longer fear it. She looked up at her mother who stood with a blank expression, just watching and holding Frankie's hand. "Mommy..." she pleaded. But, her mother said nothing.

The room was small, with a glass door that opened from the outside. One of the nurses was taking special care to hang a giant sheet of black plastic over it, covering every possible inch that light could come through. She noticed Frankie watching and gave her a sweet, comforting smile. Frankie hated her then. The other nurse was just finishing with the windows. Not a sliver of light shown through them now, and she was beginning to panic already. The only light in the room now was coming from the waiting room they sat in as the door hung open, waiting for the smiling nurse to finish.

Dr. Anderson emerged from his office a few feet away and offered them a seat across from him as he sat on a brown sofa. Her mother accepted and took a seat across from him. "OK Frankie, here's what we're gonna do kiddo," he started in his most 'kid friendly' tone. "We are going to start you off with something super easy. Today, I want you to be really, *really* brave for me. I need you to sit in that room for just two minutes. Two whole minutes. Can you do that for me?"

Frankie looked back at the room as the nurse finally finished the door. "It's dark..."

"Yeah, I know. But, look at it this way, whenever

you're all done with your two minutes, you won't have to go back in today. And, you'll get to pick out a special toy to take home." Anderson said, raising his eyebrows as though what he said were exciting enough to undertake this venture. She looked at the room again, still clutching her mother's hand. "It's OK, honey," her mother said as she gave her hand a comforting squeeze. She looked at Dr. Anderson and nodded her head, knowing full well it wouldn't take two minutes for her to regret it. "Good girl, Frankie! I'm *very* proud of you!" Anderson said. Her mother just smiled and turned her attention to the doctor as he began to speak. "Now, what's gonna happen is, today we will do two minutes, then next week we will try four, then eight, and so on until we reach an hour. By that time, she should be able to handle the dark well enough on her own," he sounded so certain as he said it, and Frankie wanted to scream. She felt like no one had listened to her at all. Ever. "Things like shouting or banging and trying to get out should be expected, especially the first time. But, no matter what, it's important not to panic. It's important to remember that it's only a couple of minutes, and it is crucial that she overcome her fear," he explained to her mother. She simply nodded and squeezed Frankie's hand. More and more Frankie hated the sound of this. It looked bad enough, did he really need to explain anymore?

Dr. Anderson gestured them to wait a moment and disappeared into his office. When he came back, he was holding a white lamb with a red bow around it's neck. "I thought since you're green bear had gotten lost, maybe you'd like this guy," it was almost a question as he handed it to her, "See, he's kinda scared of the dark too, so maybe you two could do this together? I'm sure he would like that. What do you think?"

She clutched stuffed lamb to her chest and nodded, "Thank you..." she said softly. "You're very welcome, Frankie. What's his name?" Anderson said gently as he pinched her nose. Frankie grinned and stared intently at her new friend for a moment, thinking deeply. "Yammie," she said with conviction, and nodded. Anderson smiled broadly, "What do you say we go ahead and get this over with?" He asked her encouragingly. Again, she nodded. He gave her a slight smile and took her hand, leading her to the black room. It was the longest short walk she had ever taken. A few short simple steps had turned into miles of lava and hot coals. The closer they came, the more panic overtook her, the more she fought the urge to cry, the more she wanted to run. He stopped just short and knelt down to face her. "Now, if you start to get super scared, just hug the bear really tight. Cuz, remember Frankie, he's scared too just like you are. OK? It would really make Yammie feel better I think to know that you're there to keep him safe," he was trying to comfort her. He could see on her face she was nearly frozen with fear. And maybe he was afraid for her. He sympathized with the child. In some ways, she reminded him of himself at that age. He didn't have to tell her twice as she hugged the toy so tight to her chest that he thought it's head might come off. "Don't worry, sunshine. We are going to be right here, outside this door. So, no matter what, it's going to be alright. Me and your mom will be right here," he said softly. Frankie just nodded and looked at her mother, her eyes wide and terrified as though pleading with her one final time not to make her do this. 'Two minutes', Anderson gestured to her, pursing his lips and nodding, as though to say she were tougher than she thought. Frankie hugged the lamb under her chin, pinched her eyes shut tight and stepped into the room, listening to the door close behind her.

Dr. Anderson took his seat back on the couch across from Frankie's mother. Immediately after the door had closed the girl's breathing had become heavy and rapid. She was beginning to sob and panic, and they could hear her. The small helpless whimpers of a terrified child, so convinced something was there to get her, echoed uncomfortably. "Things like this take time, Mrs. Welch. Time to get use to the idea that what she's scared of just isn't there. As a child her little mind can come up with things that you and I couldn't even imagine. And, for someone so young, hers is very, very active. Frankie just needs to adapt and get use to the dark..." he trailed off as the child began to scream. Pleading to be let out of the blackness she felt so trapped in. It was beginning to sound like someone was ripping the walls right out of the room. Scratching sounds like talons on concrete, and an indescribable thumping, as though the devil himself had a heartbeat resonated from the room. It startled even him. He began to wonder himself, irrationally of course, if perhaps her fears were real.

Mrs. Welch simply sat there, her hands folded and white knuckled on her lap, her eyes shut tight and her lips drawn inward, listening to her child in the next room, wincing and jumping at each loud bang and high pitched cry for help. Was this what happened at home when the lights went out, he wondered.

"Calm down Frankie, sweetie. Just one more minute kiddo, I promise," Anderson yelled to the closed door. The banging, scratching and screams were becoming so loud he was unsure if she even heard him. Even he was having great difficulty just sitting there allowing this to go on. It sounded like she was being thrown about the dark room like a ragdoll. And, as though furniture that wasn't even there was being thrown into walls and ripped to splinters. He wanted to run in there, pick her up and hold her and tell her it was all over and she didn't have to be afraid anymore. But, ethically, and logically, he couldn't do that.

The nurses that had blacked the room came from behind their counter, wide eyed and afraid, their hands covering their mouths, listening to the terror coming from it. They turned their gaze to the doctor as though to say 'do something.' He just shook his head at them and looked at his watch, hoping the time was up.

Close enough. With fifteen seconds left to go he stood up and jogged toward the door. Without warning it exploded outward, hurling the child into the waiting room so hard she hit the front of the sofa and rolled toward her mother. Anderson was knocked to the ground from the force at which Frankie was thrown. Screams erupted from nurses and mother alike, all rushing to see if she was still alive. Anderson stared in horror at the room she was in. The walls were shredded to ribbons from top to bottom... Every inch. The floor was blackened, smeared with blood, and carpet had been clawed and ripped up in several places. Even the ceiling sported the same damage the walls and floor had. How could a child do this...? In less than two minutes...

"Doctor!" A nurse screamed from across the room. Anderson wasted no time in leaping over furniture to the child's side. Praying to whatever God might listen that she was still alive. Anderson was taken aback by what he saw. Frankie's face, chest, back and arms were clawed to bits, her left arm was obviously broken, and she was banged up and bruised almost beyond recognition. Anderson found a pulse... A very weak pulse. "Call 911!!" He screamed so loud he could swear it was someone else saying it. The nurses both rushed for the counter to get to the phone. Frankie's mother knelt on the ground, holding her unconscious child, rocking and sobbing with a confused, bewildered, and terrified expression. Anderson stood firm though terrified for the girl, and he held his emotions well in check. Until he realized that Frankie was still holding the stuffed animal.

    It was ages ago it seemed. But, she never got over it. She had never been in a dark space again. She tore her gaze from the light switch and turned over onto her side, tossing her leg out of the blanket. She took hold of Yammie smiling at all they had gone through together over the years. She kissed his nose, hugged him tight to her chest, and began her nightly battle for sleep.

CHAPTER FIFTEEN:

ASSISTED... LIVING?

Standing at the counter waiting seemed like a chore in itself. She grew bored. The nurse that had told her to wait here a moment had been gone for almost fifteen minutes. 'Layna' was the name her tag sported. It fit her, and Frankie couldn't help but wonder who thought of it. A very pretty name.

A small breeze from an oscillating fan no more than ten inches tall waved red ribbons from it's face as it cooled a small area in the nurses station. What was taking so long? The last time she was here, it was the chipper nurse at the front desk. She had taken her straight back to see the Ingrams. This nurse was different. Not as chipper. And had, for some reason, gone back to speak to someone about her visit.

Frankie was growing impatient. Too many shadows in this place. She was uncomfortable, and confused. What was going on, she thought to herself, nearly mouthing the words.

When the nurse finally reemerged it had been nearly twenty minutes. She scuttled down the long corridor with her stout, chubby legs that seemed to be attached directly to her feet. Like someone had forgotten to give her ankles. The thick, portly hips and legs stood out on the woman, because it didn't fit with the rest of her rather small, slender frame. It looked almost like two halves of two separate women had been stacked together. She was an older woman, perhaps late forties, early fifties. And she looked worn and tired. Her light brown hair frizzed out of it's trappings on both sides, with slight hints of gray showing itself as she passed beneath the fluorescent lights. Her mouth curled downward involuntarily on her pale, passionless face, as though her years and experiences had prevented her from smiling. Frankie could only imagine. This woman, in her years of employment at this home, must have seen so much death.

"Miss Welch, I am sorry to have kept you waiting." She said impersonally. "You said you were here to see the Ingrams?" The nurse asked, showing slight hints of confusion in her near expressionless features. "And, you say you were here last week and *spoke* to them..."

"Yes." Frankie replied.

The nurse now looked at her uncertainly, rubbing her fingers along the breadth of her forehead as though she were looking for the appropriate way to say something. "Can you..." She trailed off for a moment. "Can you describe the nurse here at the desk when you came last week, ma'am?"

Frankie scratched her head then, trying to recall the nurse's features. "She was quite a bit taller than me, maybe 5'8" or so," she began, "She had sort of pinched features. Dishwater hair, about shoulder length. Maybe early twenties. A very chipper, cheerful disposition..."

The nurse was taken aback by the description. "Do you remember her name...?" Layna closed her eyes tight then, as though anticipating some ghoul to jump out at her. Frankie grew concerned. "Ma'am I'm only here to see the Ingrams. May I please..." Layna shot her eyes open and cut her off before she could finish, "Please, Miss Welch... Do you remember the nurse's name?" Frankie stared for a moment at her before responding. Layna looked genuinely worried. But, she couldn't understand why. What was going on, she wondered. "Natalie."

Frankie watched, unsure of the situation as the older woman's shoulders slumped and, she could gauge the moment her heart sank. The air in the room seemed somehow different now. Thick and heavy. Like a wool blanket had been wet down and cast over the entire place. Layna's eyes pinched shut the moment Frankie spoke the nurse's name. With a heaving sigh she opened her eyes and looked at Frankie with a confused and tired expression.

"Please Miss Welch, would you sit a moment?" Layna asked gently as she gestured to the pair of arm chairs in the waiting room near the front desk. A small, fake ficus stood between them, not big enough to block the face of the concerned nurse sitting beside her, but enough to make itself known. And, enough to be irritating.

As they sat, Layna looked down to the floor and stayed quiet for a moment, picking her fingernails in a nervous gesture. Without looking up, she began to speak quietly; so much so that Frankie barely heard her. "Natalie Harris started working here at the home nearly fifteen years ago." Frankie grew confused at that moment. Natalie looked just a few years out of twenty last week. If that were true, she would have begun work here only as a child. This made no sense... But, when Frankie opened her mouth to speak, she was immediately met with Layna's eyes, "Let me finish." She told her with the most serious tone she had ever heard.

"Natalie took care of the Ingrams herself. She insisted on it. Her shift was twelve hours, 8 AM to 8 PM, four days a week. She always worked hard, and she was an absolute joy to have around. Over time, she and the Ingrams grew very close. It was a charming sort of bond, really." Layna trailed off then, seeming to lose herself in her own mind for a moment before continuing. "The Ingrams were always so sad... They had lost their twin girls, and when they were ruled incompetent, and unable to care for themselves, they were sent here. And, it was really no mystery what happened to them. After a loss like that... Hell, anyone would lose their minds." She wandered again into her own mind for a moment, seeming now to stare off into nothing, as though she were watching a sad movie play in the distance. "All they ever did was sit at that window and stare outside. Always together, holding hands. They would just stare..." Frankie watched the slightest hint of tears form in the corner of the older woman's eyes. She wondered in that moment why she had spoken of the Ingrams and this Natalie in a past tense... And a sudden sense of dread began to claw at her chest.

"In essence, she became like another daughter to them. And, after a while... They seemed almost happy. It was a very sudden change in them. Like there was something they had to look forward to." Layna sat there, staring off at nothing as she spoke. She didn't blink. Just sat there staring, telling her story. "Every day during her shift, she would sit with them at their window, talking and laughing. Normal chit chat, like old friends make. She would make her normal rounds and go straight back to the Ingrams. The rest of us thought nothing of it. In fact, we were glad in a way, though I'm ashamed to admit it, to have them off *our* hands. But... They seemed happier." She looked down again, worrying at her fingernails the way she had a few moments earlier.

"One morning, during my rounds, I noticed them sitting there as usual. I could see between the chairs that they were holding hands like they always did. I didn't bother them. Just made my usual rounds. Nothing seemed out of the ordinary..." At that moment, the tears that clung so fiercely to her lashes, fell like small drops of rain to her blouse. But still, she didn't blink. "They were the last stop of my morning rounds. I always went to them at 10:10 AM... But, when I walked into the sitting room... It felt colder. I told them good morning like I always did. Although I was use to them never responding..." She paused again, taking in a deep, ragged breath. "That day, I just felt that something was wrong. And... When I walked up beside them, I could see the stillness in them. They had the look of death... But, they were smiling. Eyes open, staring out that window... Smiling. It was the only time I had ever seen them smile."

Frankie's eyes grew wide. What she was hearing couldn't be true. Just last week she had spoken to the Ingrams. They spoke to her. How could this be?

"We found out, after the autopsies, that Natalie had given them both a massive dose of Potassium Chloride." Layna wiped her eyes with a wadded up tissue she had pulled from her pocket. "Assisted suicide." She added coldly. "They wanted to die. I guess we all knew they did. But, it was Natalie that helped them. I suppose being as close to them as she had gotten, made her feel somehow obligated." She stared at the tissue in her folded hands for a moment, swallowing hard before looking once more to Frankie.

"Natalie was arrested... And seven weeks later, she hung herself in her jail cell, leaving behind a note explaining the whole thing... That was eight years ago, Miss Welch."

CHAPTER SIXTEEN:

A LOVEBIRD AND IT'S MATE

That night, Frankie sat in her tiny apartment, lit up like daytime, staring at nothing. Her mind, as it tended to do so often anymore, wandered over the day's events in disbelief. The Ingrams... Case closed. However confused she was, she had hope that wherever they were, they were at rest now. She didn't know how much more of this she could take. Was she mad? Even though it all added up, she still had to wonder. Was she going to end up the way Redimona had? Secluding herself away and hiding from the world?

She watched as a shadow twisted and clawed it's way across the far wall of her apartment and, however impossible it was for that to happen, she didn't even flinch. Let them come, she thought. She still didn't fully understand what the dark truly was. And, she needed to. She needed to understand why she was able to see the things she saw. Things no one else could see. These black, twisted things that came from dark places and tormented her constantly. One day, she would know. She was determined.

The ghosts she saw, however... That was something different. Was it the shadows showing her these things? Was it simply another torment? She wasn't sure of anything anymore. It seemed like the only dead she wasn't seeing, were the ones she wanted to see.

Spokane, Washington
11 years earlier

   Closed casket. She kept hearing the term throughout the funeral home. At 17, she knew what the term meant, but that didn't mean she wanted to be reminded. The funeral itself was over. But, the mass of people; some of whom she did not even recognize, still crowded the morose room as though it were a social gathering. Some means to catch up on old times.
   She sat in a folding chair in the front row, staring at the casket. It was as though she were willing it to go away. Willing it all to go back to the way it was. Back to when everything, though never OK, was always OK.
   Her father stood in a far corner of the room talking to a minister. His eyes; red and swollen seemed like glass peering out from two tired hollows. Dane stood quietly beside him, his hands folded and, his eyes just as red and glassy as their father's. She didn't know anymore how to react. She felt a sense of betrayal, mixed with shock, anger and deep, heart tearing despair.

Her mother had been walking that night, as she did every night. But, on this night, their neighbor had been drinking. It was raining, and the curve was dark. He shouldn't have been driving, but he was. He took the corner too fast and lost control of his jeep, hitting her mother, trapping her beneath the vehicle and dragging her half a mile before overturning and tumbling another forty feet, taking her along with it before finally throwing her into a tree. The medical examiner said that she hadn't felt anything. After the initial impact, she died immediately. But, Frankie could see the lie clearly in his eyes. Somehow she just knew... Her mother felt all of it.

She remembered a story her grandfather had told her once about a pair of lovebirds he watched for several years in the woods near her grandparent's home just fifty miles away in Newport. He had told her that the birds were so much in love that they depended on one another for flight. Their bond was so strong that one bird became the others wings. One day, the female bird died. Her mate, so distraught and heart broken, took flight as high up as he could go into the sky, and plummeted back down to the ground without spreading his wings, dying on impact. His love for his mate was so immense that he refused to live without her. He would say that's how much her father loved her mother. At the time, it was both a sad, and romantic story. That two beings could be so much in love that the very thought of life without one another was simply unbearable.

It was only a week before she began to notice that her father had stopped eating. His eyes looked black and sunken in, desolate and hollow, with an emptiness that one might find on the face of a puppet someone had tossed into a corner... That's what he reminded her of. He had no energy, and simply refused to leave the couch. He would just sit there. He didn't speak, he didn't sleep, he didn't eat. His features grew blank and gray, the ashen color climbing from his limbs all the way to his deeply receding hair line. And, no matter how she and Dane pleaded with him to eat... It was as though they were not even there.

Several weeks later, she and Dane were attending their father's funeral as well. They didn't have to say anything to one another. However unspoken, they each knew the other had accepted deep down, that their father died the same night their mother had. His body just took time to follow suit.

Indeed, the only dead she didn't see... Were the ones she truly wanted to...

The shadow scurrying along her wall grabbed once more at her attention, forcing her to focus on it. She could see it as it tried to take a shape in the blinding brightness of her small abode. Was it really there? How could it be? There was not room for a single shadow in this place. She even suffered through the uncomfortable heat that all of the light created in such a small space. But, still there it was... Just a small piece of blackness there on the wall, trying desperately to fight against the light and make itself whole...

'The curve was dark...' She thought...

CHAPTER SEVENTEEN:

MY NAME IS CLYDE

Abbey sat behind the reinforced glass, smacking her bright red gum and filing her nails as she had before. And still, Frankie felt her patience near fleeting the closer she came to the rude, pestiferous woman. But, she held herself well in check. Just as she had before.

Looking above Abbey, she could see the shadows in the corners form faces. The frightening things writhing and screeching, wide mouthed and hollow eyed, as though they were trapped inside the building's very structure, struggling to break free. Gaping mouths spilling blackness and widening until the jaws split at the very corners, dangling open as though they would swallow her whole. She closed her eyes against it, hoping that when she opened them again, the horrid things would be gone. Would they ever go away?

Abbey, as always, was oblivious. Wrapped up obtusely in the small television that sat adjacent to her chair. Her feet lazily propped up on the cabinet next to her desk. A moth flitted along the blinking fluorescent light, relentlessly banging itself against it like it would somehow make it inside.

"My name is Clyde." The words were clear as day. As

clear as the sound of the helmet banging against the wall. But, Clyde was nowhere to be seen this time. She stood still for a moment, staring into the empty space, listening to Clyde's repetition. The more she looked, the more she noticed dark scuff marks. They were faded, an almost orange color against the lime green fading to the piss yellow paint that peeled off the walls. A slight hint of what could have been blood descended from a splotch into a long narrow trail down to the floor.

Where was the strange, skinny man that wore the yellow helmet? That banged his head against the wall when he said his name... Where was Clyde?

The blinking of the lights were more unsettling this time. Not just because of the terrors heaving from above. But, because with each blink, she was in the dark. And, every black millisecond, brought with it some new twisted terror to plague her. Pitch, long-tongued scurriers darting this way and that; like a dance club beneath a strobe light.

Abbey, completely distracted by the small television hadn't even noticed her come in. And, didn't notice now as she stood at the counter in front of her, waiting for her attention. How she could focus on anything, even a TV, beneath the constant flickering of the fluorescent above her, was beyond Frankie. She wondered then, if Abbey even knew she was there. Likely not. However, Frankie took notice of the superfluous keyring on the far side of the wall opposite Abbey, and dismissed her last thought as minor blessing.

With a little wiggling, and some small contortionist act, she would be able to snake her arm beneath the small paper pass at the bottom of the reinforced glass, and take the ring. If she was quiet.

Frankie's eyes were on Abbey's back the whole time. Her arm got stuck for a moment, and she began to panic briefly before it slid the rest of the way through the narrow pass. She bent her arm upward and reached until it hurt, but the keys were just a hairs breadth out of her reach. She reached further. Sliding more of her arm through the small opening until it felt like a vice on her shoulder. Stifling a whimper, she was able to clutch the keys. The small tinkling noise they made as they were closed in her hand made Frankie's blood go cold and she froze there for a moment, petrified that she had been caught.

No movement from the obnoxious woman behind the desk. It was the first time Frankie was grateful that Abbey was a lazy loafer rather than a hard working do all. As she began to pull her arm back through the glass, she noticed that the lights above had begun blinking at an alarming rate. It was almost as though they would burst, or burn out at any moment. Like the dark somehow knew what it was she was now planning to do. Frankie felt panic coming on once more.

Just a bit more to go, and she was free of the receptionist's desk. But, as she felt the darkness closing in around her, she wondered now if her sudden stroke of genius was such a good thing after all. It was a burning feud inside herself whether she should continue her quest for answers, or run like hell from this place and never look back.

Twisted, evil things. Each blink revealed a hideousness marching it's way ever closer to her. It's narrow, black frame and long meatless arms ending in thin, clawed hands that looked as though they could rip her very soul from her body. Deep sunken eyes that somehow stared right into her, pulling out her every fear. Flaking skin, the color of fine charcoal seemed to tear away like ashes into a wind she could not see, as the thin strings of long pale hair blew from one side of it's face to the other.

She tried to focus on the task at hand. Tried to maintain her composure as she struggled silently to pull the keys to her side of the receptionist's desk. She was completely terrified, and unsure if she could finish this endeavor. *'Just a few more inches,'* she thought to herself.

Each flicker brought the gnarled creature closer and closer. And she began to hear whispers echoing as though they were right next to her ear. Louder and more distracting, all around her as though she were being surrounded by forces unseen. With each passing second the whispers grew more intense, a blur of noise blaring in her mind with a ferocity beyond explanation. Shrouded voices speaking over one another in incomprehensible pleas that she could not understand, but terrified her nonetheless. The whole while hearing the imperceptible Clyde introduce himself in a repetition near maddening.

Each bang of the unseen helmet against the wall, each pulsating whisper, each flicker of the lights, each step the wraith-like creature took toward her brought her closer to meeting the insanity of it all with a scream as equally mad. But, the end was in sight. With one final motion her arm was freed of it's reinforced trappings and she slumped noiselessly to the floor with the keys in her hand, covering her ears to block the sounds and pinching her eyes shut so tight it hurt, as though these actions would somehow bring her comfort.

She sat there for only a moment before realizing that it was quiet. No banging of Clyde's helmet. No whispers. When she mustered the courage to open her eyes, the light was buzzing and steady. No flickering. Only the jutting rhythm of the moth banging loudly against it. And Abbey, as obliviously ignorant of her surroundings as ever.

Frankie took in a long breath, closed her eyes and held it a moment before slowly allowing the much needed air to escape. She realized now that she was on the right track... And, something was trying to stop her. She leaned her head against the wall just beneath the glass, staring up at the blinding fluorescent light, simply appreciating it's steady glow. Was she really about to do this? Too late to turn back now...

She didn't stand up. She crawled to the door next to the receptionist's enclosure, just in case Abbey

decided suddenly to do her job. The door lead to the
dimly lit hallway... The one she dreaded. It took all
the courage she could muster to turn the key and
open the door. And even more to crawl through it and
close it behind her. She leaned against it for a
moment, trying to forget the scent of old urine and
turpentine. This place was hell. Paint flakes from the
wall stuck to the back of her shirt, making her skin
itch and burn. Her hands, still sore and wrapped from
her endeavor at the Ingram's home, made crawling
through this place even more difficult. And, at that
point she became paranoid about even touching the
floor. Then grew ridiculously concerned about what
type of infection she may get from this disgusting
place, running down a list of germs and bacteria in
her mind. When she stood up, her head began to
swim. Her heart was still racing, and even through the
fear she had an unexplainable determination to keep
going. She couldn't believe she was doing this.

   She couldn't help but stare into the blackness down
the corridor as though it would lurch forth and take
her. Her first step wasn't as difficult as she thought it
would have been. But, it gradually grew more difficult
as she kept on. She was unpleasantly aware of the
floor's texture beneath her feet. Squishing and
crunching with each step she took. She swallowed
hard, balling her fists and holding them tight against
her thighs as she slowly advanced at a painfully
reluctant pace.

   Decrepit doors adorning rooms cloaked in darkness

lined both sides of the hall. They seemed empty, though she could feel eyes on her with each door she passed. Small windows the size of dinner plates showed no sign of life inside the tiny rooms, but she dared not move any closer to them to peer in.

A loud bang caused her to start and jump, gasping for breath. It came from one of the rooms just ahead of her. "My name is Clyde." She heard. "My name is Clyde." She couldn't take much more of this. Whoever, or whatever 'Clyde' was... He seemed to be following her.

The closer she came, the clearer she could see the light flickering on and off in the room emitting the noise. Each time the flickering lit the room, a presence would appear in the small window. She didn't have to wonder who it was, or what it was anymore. Every glint revealed the face of a man. Blood ran down both sides of his head and face, trailing in long thin lines down his neck, and into his white shirt. His yellow-orange helmet was badly dented, and scuffed on either side. His face was almost child-like, though he looked to be nearly thirty. She felt a sense of innocence from him.

His palm pressed against the window as he looked to her, and back to his hand, in an eager gesture that revealed more of his nature than she expected. His smile was crooked, and a stream of drool ran from the corner of his mouth and down his chin, giving her the sudden urge to gently wipe it away. His eyes; big and full of wonder, like those of a young boy coaxed her, darting from her to his outstretched hand and back again. Over and over.

Though she was hesitant, she found her arm reaching out, her hand opening to fit against the glass in a gesture to somehow meet the palm on the other side. A motherly sense seemed to wash over her. An unbearable urge to hold this man; to comfort him and tell him everything would be okay, gripped at her until her throat hurt. Did it show on her face, she wondered. When her hand finally met the glass she was completely taken aback by what would happen.

In a flash of white she found herself huddled in a gray haze. The buzzing of people all around her bringing a ringing to her ears that seemed to grow louder and louder. She felt like a small child now, helpless in her surroundings. But, she recognized her surroundings. However gray and muddled her environment now was, it still revealed the same building she had been in only a moment ago. But, it was new. Almost pristine. The droning noise in her head made by the people around her was near deafening.

One man stood only inches away, swaying back and forth in front of a window. Another, rather disheveled looking sat at a table not far away, eating playing cards. There were so many people here. People whose minds did not seem to be their own. She didn't belong here. Two orderlies stood in a far corner smoking cigarettes while a medley of cartoons played on a TV above her. She began to bang her head against the wall she crouched against, trying to make the noise subside. She didn't like it here. And, she began to wish she were safe at home. It was too loud here. She covered her ears, but it didn't help. So loud. Every noise was it's own torment to her. What was happening? She began to panic. She needed something familiar to keep with her. Something she knew. "My name is Clyde."

Reality hit her like a ton of bricks and she jumped back. She stared into the child-like eyes of the ghost holding his hand against the small pane of glass, still beckoning her to it. Did she dare? It was such a real experience... She found herself frightened and, very reluctant to touch the glass where Clyde's hand pressed eagerly against the other side.

"What happened to you...?" She whispered, near sobbing. The apparition looked down for a moment before leaning his head on the glass, seemingly plagued by his memories. His hand still firmly in place, he opened his eyes and looked at her. There was a very different look in his eyes now. Fear, longing, pain. He set his glance once more to his hand, and again to her. He needed to share it with her. Needed someone to know. She hesitated only a moment before summoning the courage from deep within her to touch the glass once more.

Like a shot she found herself crouched by a wall again. But, this wall was different. Somehow colder than the last. She found herself in the dark... Alone and terrified. It was a new kind of fear. A new kind of panic. Not just of the dark around her... But, something else. She felt the tears, hot on her face as she whimpered and cried. Her cuticles burned and stung from anxiously biting her nails down to the bed. This was a terror she had never known before. But, it wasn't because of the room she found herself in. No. She knew *that* fear. This fear... Was of being let *out* of the room. But, why?

Again, she began to bang her head against the wall. It didn't hurt like before. Something cushioned the blow now. Soft and somehow comforting to her. "My name is Clyde." She clung to the sentence as though she might forget. "My name is Clyde."

Footsteps, distant but heavy began descending down the corridor outside. She froze then, gripped in sheer terror of what was to come. The cadence was uneven but steady in pace. Two of them were coming. Her panic grew with each approaching thud of the orderlies boots. Why was she so afraid...?

She gritted her teeth against the sound of a key sliding into the lock on the door. Light spilled into the black room when it was swung open, blinding her for a moment. Laughter emanated from the hallway as the two orderlies shared a story of sexual conquest. A horrid sound, their laughter. So near evil that she had to wonder if the devil himself were embodied there. When the figures emerged from the corridor, she stared up at her two worst nightmares. Rogers, a potbellied drunk that was even too arrogant to hide his alcoholism at work. And Norton, a life long bully that applied for a position here because he simply couldn't resist the cornucopia that provided his favorite pass time; the utter torment of the weak and helpless.

"Alright dummy, let's go. Time for your therapy." Rogers said mockingly. He and Norton both began to chuckle at the word. Therapy. She didn't move. Just stared up at them frozen, her knees tucked in her arms, terrified of what was to come. Norton smacked her on the side of the helmet, sending her head slamming against the wall so hard it made her neck hurt. "Come on, brainless! Let's go! We ain't got all damn day!"

She let out a loud protest at the abuse and was met with a hard kick to her thigh from Norton, and another smack from Rogers. "Get up!" Rogers demanded. She felt helpless. Weak and afraid. She slid upward against the wall slowly, flinching and shielding herself from more blows she feared would fall. "I want my mommy." She managed in a small, shaking voice. They burst out then in bellowing laughter. "Thirty years old, and he wants his fuckin' mommy!" Norton said, near doubling over with laughter. Rogers, still in a chuckle slammed her against the wall with one hand, and began slapping the side of her head with the other. "Your mommy don't want you, idiot boy. Your ass belongs to us now. Get use to it." He then flung her towards the open door with enough force that she almost fell to the ground.

She began to sob uncontrollably as she made her way down the long corridor. Dread filled her every sense as the two men guided her further and further along. They began to chortle at her fear and sorrow; the more she wept, the more they seemed to enjoy themselves. They stopped abruptly at the door marked 'Staff Only' in bright red letters. Rogers opened it, and Norton pushed her through so hard she stumbled, falling down the flight of stairs leading to the basement.

"So, you know that hot little piece of ass in the Crisis Ward?" She heard Norton say in a near muddled voice. Her head felt like it was swimming. The fall down the stairs made her feel like she was under water. She wanted to sleep.

"You mean the uh... Forever virgin nun in street clothes... uh... The cutter. Shit, what's her name?" Rogers rubbed his forehead as though he would be able to find what he was looking for there. They descended the stairs in strides as they carried on their vulgar conversation. She felt like she shouldn't hear what they were saying. As though hearing it would make her like they were. Bad.

"Fuck, I don't know her name!" Norton replied with a chuckle. They stopped on the bottom step, just short of her to finish their conversation. "I know she ain't a virgin now though." Norton laughed when he said it, as though he were extraordinarily proud of himself.

"You fucked her? Oh man, tell me you fucked her!"

Rogers said in a tone nearing excitement. She covered her ears, but it didn't help. She could still hear them as though she hadn't moved her hands at all.

"Well, hell yes I did. And boy, lemme tell you... That precious little pink was *sweet*! Mmm mmm *mmm*! She fought for a while, but she knew she wanted it. I'm gonna be having fun with that for a good long time, boy!" Norton gloated, beaming with pride. She found herself disgusted. She was nauseated by these two repulsive animals.

Rogers bellowed in laughter and slapped Norton on the back, congratulating him on his conquest. He then put his hands on his hips and stared down at her, cocking his head to the side. "Well... Let's take this dummy to get zapped and move on, shall we?"

They each took a firm, painful grip on her arms and lifted her to her feet. Her head ached and throbbed, and she could feel something hot and sticky running out of her helmet and down the sides of her face. It didn't take long before her dread increased tenfold. They opened a door and walked her through, picking her up and laying her down on a cold, steel gurney.

"Here's your victim." Rogers said jokingly. A woman, in a nurses uniform stepped forward and looked down at her with loving, comforting eyes. Her vision blurred and faded in and out, but she did not feel threatened by this woman. The nurse's look then changed. Comfort and safety turned suddenly to concern. "Why is he bleeding?" She asked as Rogers and Norton stood, cross armed on the other side of the room, talking.

Rogers looked at her blankly, and before he could speak, Norton interjected, "The jackass slams his fuckin' head into walls. What do you think is gonna happen?" She narrowed her eyes and spoke in a gentle, but assertive tone then, "Around me, you *will* watch your language." Norton and Rogers both laughed then, and went back to their conversation.

She removed the helmet gently, and placed it on the table beside her. When she did, she saw the massive wounds caused by the orderlies abuse. Blood crusted in the patient's hair and seeped in small pools onto the steel table. She stood shocked, and shook her head. She quickly moved to the phone on her right and put it to her ear. But, before she could even push the button for the infirmary, Norton was at her back. He pulled out a small pocket knife and placed it firm against her throat, pressing his cheek against hers and whispering gruffly. "Just do what you do, pretty girl. No need for all that. Just do what you do. Trust me... It's a lot better than the alternative." He said smugly before nibbling her earlobe.

She stared down at her with remorse and pity. Sorry for what she was being forced to do. "It will kill him." She whispered to the man holding the knife against her throat. Norton was rubbing his face against her hair now, smelling her and gently licking at her ear. "So?" He replied. "Do what I said, and I'll leave you alone. Understand?" He pressed the knife against her a bit harder, and she gasped. "OK... OK, I'll do it."

She whimpered. Norton then reached with his free arm and unplugged the service phone at both ends, wrapping the cord around his hand. "Then we don't have a problem, do we pretty girl?" He whispered in her ear before slithering his tongue in it and releasing her. She looked like she might vomit.

He crossed the room and nonchalantly resumed his conversation with Rogers as though nothing had transpired. Frankie stared up at the nurse in terror, unable to move. Tears formed in the woman's eyes as she began to strap Frankie to the table, each restraint uniformly buckled down. The buzzing of a machine clicked on. A familiar sound, and yet not. Gradually, the humming became louder, like an electrical song meant to lull one into sleep. Nausea swept over her in waves as her vision blurred and dimmed unsteadily. The nurse reappeared with a small rod wrapped generously in white cloth, placing it firmly between Frankie's teeth. Blinking slowly, she could only stare up at the nurse, and plead with her eyes alone, that she not do this.

She stared down at her for a moment, stroking her hair. Her tears fell onto Frankie's forehead in small drops of complete and unfathomable sadness. "I'm so sorry..." She wept. "Please... Please forgive me." It was the last thing she heard before cold, wet metal was placed against her temples. Lightning shot through her. And, then there was only blackness.

She woke in the dark. Pain shot through her like thunder. It was almost impossible to move. She was so weak. So tired. "Let me out..." She whimpered so low it was near inaudible. It was the only way to get home. The only way to get free... She had to get out. If she stayed in this dark room alone, she knew she would die. The tiny light emitting from the small window of the door was her only guide to salvation now. She needed help. Her head was exploding with pain, and she could feel blood trickling down her face and neck. If she could just get out, she would be OK. She would be free. She would be saved.

The helmet felt so heavy now as she crawled toward the door. It felt like it weighed her down. Fatigue was beginning to overtake her. She made it across the tiny room to the door, only to find it was locked. She could not get out. She slumped against the metal and began to shout as loudly as she could, "Help me!!" But, no matter how she screamed and shouted, there was no response. "Help me! Let me out! I need help! Please!!" Nothing.

Her whole body was wracked with pain. So much pain. She did not want to move, fearing if she did, her bones would simply turn to dust. "I want my mommy..." It was the last words she could muster before blackness took her.

Frankie jumped back from the door and stared at Clyde, her tears no longer waiting as they ran like a river down her face. She slid down the wall across from him and wept uncontrollably. How this poor man had suffered... How could anyone be so cruel? She felt sorrow, rage, and unbearable hatred welling up inside of her. Now she knew why he had shown her this. It seemed like hours passed before she regained control of herself and stood back up.

Clyde was still there, blinking on and off with the lights. His hand no longer pressed against the glass, but now he simply looked at her with those sweet, innocent eyes. She stepped forward and looked at him gently, her eyes wet and red from sobbing. 'Let me out...' It went through her thoughts in a constant whisper. She slid the key into the lock on his door and opened it. The tall, thin man stepped uncertainly out of the small room, looking around him in wonder. A halo of light surrounded him and he smiled. The most precious smile she had ever seen. Like a lost child coming home.

He turned to her then and looked lovingly into her eyes, taking tiny, unsure steps toward her. Her tears fell once more as she placed her hands on his face, gently holding it. He was really there... She felt him. His skin, smooth as a child's, was warm beneath her touch. "Go home..." She whispered. He bent down and pressed his forehead against hers in a gesture that could only be described as an embrace. His eyes closed as a tear fell down his cheek. "My name is Clyde."

He turned then, and began to walk away. His awkward gait had a sense of certainty to it now, as though he knew where to go. She watched with mixed emotions as he disappeared in a flash of brilliant light.

CHAPTER EIGHTEEN:

BREAKING OUT BATHORY

She sat with her back against the wall across from Clyde's room. The door hung open, and the room was empty. She had to wonder if what just happened was real. She sat lost in her thoughts for some time, unaware of herself, or her surroundings. Lost in oblivion. A child... Trapped in the body of a man. She had to wonder how he even ended up there. The poor thing. Her eyes stung, and her head ached almost as much as her heart did.

She had to pull herself together; needed to focus on the task at hand. Clyde was not what she came here for. She was here for Danika Bathory.

She stood up slowly, her eyes pinned to the empty room in front of her. She had a sense of disbelief mingling with a sense of inescapable sorrow. But, she had work to do. She came here for answers, and she wasn't leaving without them. Not this time.

It took longer than anticipated to peel her eyes from Clyde's room. She almost didn't want to. She knew he was gone. Knew he was finally at peace... But still, she somehow felt that if she walked away, she was abandoning him. She turned, gave the room a last look, and said goodbye to Clyde before resuming her hesitant walk toward the darkness of the corridor.

It wasn't a long walk. However, the pitch blackness ahead made it seem like miles. Even though, with each step, the darkness moved away, the frightening thought crossed her mind more than once asking, what if it didn't this time?

The frayed orange sign immediately caught her attention, making her stop so abruptly she could have screeched. 'Bingo,' she thought. Familiar numbers scrawled on a piece of badly decomposing paper read 3122564 and, the small glass window showed a room lit up like daytime.

Her hands began to shake. Was she really doing this? Fear gripped her in remembrance of the last visit she had made to Danika Bathory. However insane the woman may be, she also made sense.

She could barely keep hold of the keys as she shuffled through them to find once more the one that opened the doors on the main floor. Her hands shook so uncontrollably that she fumbled the ring and dropped them to the ground with a loud clinking sound that seemed to echo throughout the entire building. She closed her eyes and cursed herself silently before bending to pick them back up.

When she stood, she was met with the pale, white face of Danika Bathory, bleak and expressionless, staring intently through the small square window of her door. Frankie screamed and slammed her back into the wall behind her, losing her breath when she did. She gripped at her chest, hoping that it would somehow slow her heartbeat enough to breathe again.

Danika seemed unmoved. She simply stood there at the door, staring at her as though she knew why she was there. As though she were waiting.

However disheveled the woman was, she was actually quite lovely. At seventy, she looked no older than half that, save for the matted, mangled white hair that hung in her face. Her ivory white skin showed nearly no sign of her age. But, her eyes reflected years of torment that had yet to be forgotten. Her age showed there... And yet, nowhere else. She was beautiful, even at seventy.

Danika simply stood there, waiting for Frankie to regain her bearings. Frankie hesitated a moment, unsure of what she should do; open Danika's door... Or run like hell as far from this place as she could get. She had come here with a fierce determination. A determination to get the answers she had sought for so long. A determination that she would *not* leave this place without them. And, she *knew* Danika had the answers she so desperately needed. She knew she would leave here with an understanding of some kind.

It took every ounce of courage she could summon to peel herself away from the tattered wall at her back. The keys in her hand were gripped so hard she could feel their teeth digging into her already sore and tender fingers. Her eyes only left Danika's long enough to gaze at the lock on her door before sliding in the key. It seemed as though every tumbler that folded under the metal was loud enough to burst her eardrums. When the door finally opened, Danika looked intently at her rescuer. "I wondered when you would come back." She said softly. "I hadn't expected you so soon."

Frankie looked at her unknowingly, and uncertain of what to do now. She knew she needed Danika... But, now what? She almost laughed out loud at herself, realizing that she hadn't planned this far ahead. Danika hadn't moved from her brightly lit room, which confused Frankie even further. She simply stared out the door now, scanning the corridor with features near saddened. As though she anticipated, but accepted some ominous truth. "You came for answers, child..." Her eyes never left the length of the black corridor as she quietly spoke. "Let's go get them."

The moment Danika stepped out of her room and into the dimly lit hall, every shadow around them seemed to come to life. Lurching and writhing from every direction, as though desperately trying to reach out and take her. She took Frankie's hand and gently squeezed it, making Frankie wince. Danika slowly closed her eyes to the screeching darkness that seemed to rage against the confines of the shadows to consume her.

With each step the dark seemed to take new form. Twisting in the black like some tormented wraith fighting in the shadows to stake claim on her soul. The horrific spectacle made her think of starving wolves on a helpless rabbit. Still, Danika, with her closed eyes, walked slowly in their narrow path of light. Her resolve unshaken by the terror, clawing and swiping, twisted and hungry. For a moment, Frankie was stirred by her courage. She said nothing, but kept hold of the older woman's hand, and followed quietly.

At the end of the corridor stood a large steel door marked 'B LVL 1.' She couldn't help but notice that there were no elevators in this wretched place. "Give me the keys." Danika spoke softly. Her voice was as steady as her resolve. Frankie silently obeyed, handing over the large ring, her eyes fixed on the walls around them. She focused in horrid disbelief at what was happening. She had seen it before... But, never this way. They had never seemed so hungry before. Why did they want her so?

The ghastly figures clawing across the walls wailed and howled their demanding from black, slobbering masses that should have been mouths, but somehow were not. Frankie feared that with one misstep into the slightest dark, that she and Danika would be snatched into nothingness. She then decided it best that she paid obsessive attention to her footsteps.

The door groaned open and Danika advanced, her bare feet tapping lightly on the steps as Frankie followed close behind. The bottom revealed a small room with only one door marked 'Records.' Frankie felt her confusion growing into frustration. What was she doing, she wondered. Had she made a mistake coming here after all?

"No, child... Not a mistake. You wanted answers, and you will have them." Danika said solemnly.

Frankie found herself standing frozen at that. Had she said it aloud? No. She knew she hadn't. What the hell was going on?

Danika rested her head against the glass on the door. Seeming almost happy to be there. Like there was a long lost love waiting for her within. She released Frankie's hand and ran her own down the glass, leaving a clean trail where her fingers had been. Cobwebs and dust fell into her pale hair as she caressed the door with her cheek. Frankie stood confused. This woman truly *was* mad.

Frankie hadn't heard the door unlock, but Danika opened it, revealing a room covered in dust and cobwebs. The place was empty, save for a few cabinets and chests, neglected and decaying. The light was sparse, but there was enough to reach a small chest just nearing the center of the room.

Danika stood beneath a light that dangled precariously from it's trappings. Frankie had to wonder then, how it was still functional. It looked as though at any moment, it would snap loose and knock Danika to the ground. But, she didn't even seem to notice as she wrestled a drawer of the chest open, a cloud of dust coughing from it as it gave.

"Here, child." She said gently as she pulled a brown folder from it's confines and laid it atop the chest. "Everything you need to know is here."

Frankie stared for a moment at the decrepit file. She questioned whether or not then that she really wanted to know... Was this the end of her journey? Were her

questions truly going to be answered... And, was there a way to make it all stop? She stared unsure at the deep imprints of Danika's slender finger tips in the thick dust adorning the folder, and stepped forward, noting momentarily the slightest of smiles crossing the older woman's lips.
   Patient No: 3122564
   Danika E. Bathory

   Frankie opened the thick folder, and immediately fell two sheets of loose document. Both of which would change her life completely.

CERTIFICATE OF LIVE BIRTH

Given Names: Claudius Clyde Grace
Last Name: Bathory

Date Of Birth: November 16, 1970
Facility: Shady Acres Asylum
Place Of Birth: Spokane, Spokane County, Washington
Time Of Birth: 10:39 PM
Sex: Male

Mother's Maiden Name: Danika Elizabeth Bathory
Father's Name: Unknown

   Frankie looked at Danika, her eyes wide and glossed with tears. "Clyde... Was your son...?"

Danika swayed to and fro, her arms cradled as though she were holding a baby. Her eyes were closed and a broad smile crossed her face. She looked so happy... She then simply looked at Frankie, "Keep going..." She whispered.

Stapled carelessly to the Birth certificate, was also a Death certificate...

CERTIFICATE OF DEATH

Given Names: Claudius Clyde Grace
Last Name: Bathory

County Of Death: Spokane County
Date Of Death: November 16, 1999
Hour Of Death: Unknown
Sex: Male
Aged: 29 Years
Race: White

Birth Date: November 16, 1970
Birth Place: Shady Acres Asylum
Place Of Death: Shady Acres Asylum

Cause Of Death: Blunt Force Trauma, Starvation, Neglect, EST. (Electro-shock Therapy)

Mother: Danika E. Bathory
Father: Unknown

Method Of Disposition: Cremation
Identifiable: Dental
Reason: Remains were undiscovered for several weeks.
When the patient was found, the body was in an
advanced state of decomposition.

Frankie wanted to choke Danika then. How could
she allow this to happen to her own son?
"He stayed in my room with me for the first few
years... But, after a while, they began to see that he
had learning disabilities, and put him in another
ward. They took my boy from me..." Danika's eyes
began to look far away. Tears welled up in them like
shards of glass, stinging until they were given release.
"Eventually, they allowed me to stay in the same ward
with him, but not the same room. So... After they
took him from me... I never saw him again." She
closed her eyes then. "Not until they killed him."
It gave her a small sense of understanding... But, why
the cruelty? Why didn't anyone do anything about
this place? "Danika I-" She was cut off then. "You
wanted answers, girl... Keep going." Danika asserted.
Frankie was hesitant. The second document was face
down, askew of the thick file folder. She nearly fainted
when she picked it up and read it.

CERTIFICATE OF LIVE BIRTH

Given Names: Frankie Lynn
Last Name: Bathory

Date Of Birth: April 9, 1985
Facility: Shady Acres Asylum
Place Of Birth: Spokane, Spokane County,
Washington
Time Of Birth: 12:01 AM
Sex: Female

Mother's Maiden Name: Danika Elizabeth Bathory
Father's Name: Unknown

She felt sick. She stumbled, and eventually sat down with the paper still in her hand. She leaned against the chest and watched as her tears hit the filthy floor beneath her.

"They took you too," Danika whispered. "They wouldn't even let me say goodbye. They just stole you away before I ever even had a chance to hold you." Frankie just sat quietly, listening to her. They told me that you were with a good family, that would love and care for you... I got *some* comfort out of that."

She was shaking. In shock. These weren't the answers she needed. This was not what she was looking for. "But, it is, child. These facts, will lead you to the truth you seek." Danika said, as though reading her thoughts. "Understand, girl... I've been in this place since 1969. I've had two children since then and I've never left this place." Danika seemed to lose her train of thought then. Frankie looked up at her as a shadowed hand reached into the light and caressed the older woman's face like a lover. *"Danika..."* A long and sensual whisper from the shadow as it suffered the light to touch her. The black, flaking hand began to puff and smoke, cracking and sizzling in the light in a manner that looked most painful. Danika leaned into it, as though it was something familiar, and longed for. Frankie shot up and pulled at Danika's tattered gown, jerking her away from the dark. The shadow seemed to scream and growl in protest. And, for a moment, Frankie was afraid. But, more than afraid, she was furious. And, becoming more so by the minute. In a split second her life had completely been turned upside down. Everything she had known was a lie. All of it. There were other answers she needed now.

In that moment, Danika snapped back into her senses, and Frankie's voice rang in her ears. "What happened then?!" She shouted, shaking the woman. "Who is my father?! An orderly? A doctor? *Who?!* Tell me!"

Danika stared at her then, alarmed at Frankie's sudden outburst. "Your father..." She whispered in a hushed tone. "Your father..." She repeated. "Your father..." Frankie shook her again, harder this time. "Just tell me!!" Again Danika looked at her in shock before she spoke. "Your father is not of this world," She turned her head to the shadows as she said it. "He's of theirs." Frankie's shock increased tenfold then, and she found herself staring into the darkness with Danika. She didn't know what to think. What to believe. Was Danika truly insane? Was Frankie herself insane?

She simply stood there, staring at Danika in disbelief and horror. It couldn't be true, could it? It couldn't be. She *had* to be crazy. But, the more Frankie thought about what she'd been told... The more sense her whole life seemed to make. Everything she saw. Everything she heard. It was all real. And, this was why.

Danika pulled her eyes away from Frankie turned, just out of reach of the blackness. It seemed to churn and thrash before her, like it ached for her. Like it would eat her alive. "I always thought it was so strange," She began. Her tone was soft, mild and almost comforting. "The only man in this world that ever truly loved me..." She hesitated before finishing, staring into the shadows as she spoke. "Was never a part of *this* world." She chuckled lightly, her slender fingers gently touching her lips. Frankie listened in wonder, unknowing of where this new truth would lead her. If anywhere.

"I have hidden in the light from him for so long..." She continued, and Frankie watched the shadowed hand reach once more for her. "Danika!" Frankie warned, afraid that the dark would snatch her away. "It's alright, Frankie." She said gently. "I don't belong here... Not anymore." She smiled at her then, reaching out to touch Frankie's face. "He needs me. He's calling me." She said to her with a comforting smile. Danika seemed happy then. Like she knew where she belonged. "Please no," Frankie pleaded, "Don't leave me alone now. Please."

Danika brushed a lock of hair from Frankie's face and smiled at her lovingly. "All of your answers are in that folder." She said. Frankie turned to the file on the chest, wondering what answers could possibly be kept in that infernal bearer of torment. Had she not already been given enough grief from it, she thought to herself. And, as she thought it, she heard Danika scream in such a way that she would never forget. It sounded as though she were being dragged to the depths of hell itself. When Frankie shot back toward the sound, the darkness was still, and Danika was gone.

CHAPTER NINETEEN:

NEW TRUTHS AND OLD LIES

Frankie sat in the floor of her apartment, staring at an old, tattered, brown file folder, weeping uncontrollably. At some point she might even open it and look inside. Her thoughts scattered about the realizations she now had to live with. 'All of your answers are in that folder.' It repeated in her mind over and over.

It was dawn before she was finally able to get a grip on her emotions. And, she began to realize that the only people that had any information about the things she experienced, were gone. She started to wonder then, if it was her fault. As die hard as she had been to get her answers, now that they sat before her, she hadn't even opened the folder to seek them out. She found herself riddled with confusion and sorrow. She was in shock. Maybe she *did* belong locked away.

She wasn't aware of how long she sat there, staring at the bulking, closed file as though it didn't even exist. Only that she knew less about herself now, than she had when she began searching for answers. She was tired. Frustrated. Weary. Her struggle had brought her nothing but heartache and grief. But, after everything she, and others had gone through to help her... How could she stop now?

She forced herself to her feet, her body heavy and tired. She was exhausted. She peeled off her clothes, one filthy article at a time, as she walked to her shower. She turned on the hot water, without turning on the cold, and stood in front of the mirror, watching it fog up. She stared for a moment at her distorted features and wondered, was this how everyone saw her?

Her thin, shoulder length brown hair frayed and fell into her face as she yanked out the dirty tie that held it in place. Debris from the asylum walls that had clung so desperately to the locks, now fell to her bare skin. 'Who was she,' she thought to herself.

Her eyes narrowed as she wiped the mist from the mirror and stared at her reflection with frustration. "I am Frankie Welch." She said out loud. "Frankie didn't start looking for answers about her origins. She started looking for answers about the darklings!" She said with resolve. She raised her chin with a new sense of self, and nodded to her reflection. She stepped into the shower without having taken notice... That her reflection didn't nod back. Instead it remained where it was, peering about it's glass encasement at the light surrounding it, and then banging ferociously at it in a mad struggle to break through.

Frankie simply washed herself clean of any reminders of Shady Acres, relishing the warmth of the water falling over her face. She stood there for several moments, allowing the hard rain of heat to relax her sore muscles, before turning the water off with a loud squeak. She stepped out of the shower and wrapped a towel around herself, taking another to her hair. As the towel soaked in the moisture from her hair, she couldn't help but note that the mirror was oddly free of mist. Her shower had been long enough, and hot enough, that the mirror should have a thick, wet coat of it. 'Strange,' she thought, dismissing it and heading to the living area for clothes, coffee, and the dreaded file.

She simply donned a black tank top and a pair of black and pink plaid pajama pants, letting her wet hair hang loose, as she had positively *no* intention of leaving her home today. Comfort was a long forgotten, and well deserved luxury at this point.

She stood in the kitchen, sipping her coffee from her 'Footloose' mug; her favorite cup, sporting the ever gorgeous Ren McCormick in his white tank top and second skin blue jeans. She had her back against the counter, staring across her living room, slash bedroom, slash office, at the folder laying in the middle of the floor. A new sense of determination washing suddenly over her. 'All of your answers are in that folder,' Danika's voice repeated itself in her head. She had lost count of how many times that very sentence haunted her since she'd left that awful place.

With her free hand she pushed herself away from the counter and headed toward the file. She heaved it up in her arm and plopped down on the sofa, setting her coffee mug down on the transparent glass table in front of her. When she tried to open the leather tie holding the file closed, it simply crumbled and fell apart, releasing the accordion folder filled with weathered papers, cassette tapes, drawings and dust.

She pulled out her father's old tape recorder and sat back down. For a moment, she thought she heard someone scratching, or scurrying through her apartment. She looked around with her brow furrowed, but saw nothing. She's just hearing things, she thought, not believing it for a moment. She decided to focus herself, and ignore the noises for now.

She popped open the recorder door and inserted a cassette marked, 'February 18th, 1969. Therapy Session 1. Danika E. Bathory.' She pushed play, and listened intently as the static sliced through the silence.

" *The date is March twenty-first, 1970.*
This is Dr. Edwin Haskins. Therapy session number one. Patient name, Danika Elizabeth Bathory. Aged, twenty-seven years. Caucasian female.

Danika, my dear, would you mind stepping away from the lamp and joining me here?"

His voice sounded quite veteran. She pictured a man with white hair, balding on top. A beard and mustache, neatly kept. Maybe a pair of thick glasses to complete the image. His voice was very calming. Comforting. Almost like Dr. Anderson's voice, but deeper, and more weathered.

"*I need the light.*" Danika's voice came. She sounded panicked. Her breath fell heavy and uneven, full of fear.

"That's quite alright, dear. You see? There is a lamp right here beside the chair. Would you like me to turn it on for you?" He was kind. It seemed he genuinely wanted to help her.

"Yes... Yes, please." The panicked voice of Danika Bathory seemed to calm then. Her breath seemed to slow, and steady itself as a switch clicked. Only then did Frankie hear Danika's breath draw closer to the recorder. She heard the fabric of a chair rustle and settle, and then the doctor spoke.

"There now, isn't that better, my dear? It must be more comfortable than crouching there in the corner?"

"Yes... Thank you." Danika's voice came.

"So..." Haskins began in a soft tone. *"Danika Bathory... That's quite a profound name. Any relation to the great countess?"* He asked. His tone was even, soft, and reassuring. Indeed, he reminded her of Dr. Anderson. Just a more veteran, gruff version of him.

"Danika...?" He repeated. There was only static for a moment.

"Yes..." Danika's voice reluctantly fell. *"She is my grandmother..."*

"Four or five times great, I'm assuming." The doctor chuckled lightly when he said it. Danika did not reply. Haskins cleared his throat and continued the session. *"With a family history like that, I imagine you've had a lot of unwanted attention, yes?"* The remark hung on the air like fog; thick and heavy. It would be several moments before he would get a

response from her.

"Some..." Was the only reply to his query. It was as though she were far away somewhere. Even over a recorded conversation, Frankie could tell that Danika was in the room with Haskins, and yet she was not.

"Would you care to discuss it?" Haskins asked.

There was a long pause then. Frankie noted the heaviness of the atmosphere surrounding the conversation. She found it rather chilling that she could sense it, even over a tape recording. She could have been standing in the room with them.

"She made a promise to someone..." Danika said in a tone so quiet, she could barely be heard. *"One she had no right to make."* She finished.

"What promise is that, Danika?" His question was once more met with a drawn out silence, before Danika met him with a reply.

"Her descendants." Was the only answer she gave him.

"Would you care to elaborate on that, my dear?" Haskins asked kindly.

"No." She responded abruptly.

Haskins noted her tone and moved on.

"Your file says you're pregnant. Congratulations!" He said. Frankie could hear the smile in his voice as he said it. There was a long silence then, and heaviness once again fell over the atmosphere. *"This is a good thing... is it not, Miss Danika?"* His sweet, comforting voice hinted now at concern.

"It has to be a boy..." She responded. Her voice

breathy now, as though she were frightened. *"He won't take it if it's a boy."*

"The father?" Haskins asked. Just silence. *"Why, Miss Danika? Why wouldn't the father want the child if it's a boy?"* Again, only silence. She could hear him sit forward in his chair. *"Danika dear... You must understand, I can't help you if you don't talk to me. And, I want to help you. I want you to be able to leave this place, and raise your child..."* Haskins paused only for a moment. *"The man that brought you here, Mr. Kurt Janos... is he the father?"* He was answered with a loud clap and hysterical laughter from Danika.

"No, no!" She replied, still chuckling a bit. *"I've known Kurt since we were kids. He is like my brother. He isn't..."* Her voice trailed off then into silence.

"Danika, dear..." Haskins' voice held traces of uncertainty now as he spoke gently to her. *"Can you tell me who the father is?"*

The ensuing silence was long. Static crackled over the speaker like a camp fire spitting and popping. Frankie began to wonder if the tape were finished... And, then the answer broke through the silence.

"Mallard Veephit..." Danika whispered in a frightened tone. The terror in her voice was more than evident as she said the name. Frankie quickly picked up her laptop and did a search for this Mallard Veephit. The results returned no leads.

And, then something happened. Frankie couldn't tell what it was. But, there was something clearly happening in the room.

"Danika! Danika, calm down, dear! It's alright. You're safe here!" She heard Haskins' voice growing in earnest and pure worry. *"Danika!"* Danika began to scream and weep.

"He comes in the dark! It's the dark! He's the dark!" She screamed in horror between sobs.

"I need the orderlies, now! Now!" Haskins shouted. And then silence.

Frankie simply sat there for a while, staring down at the tape recorder. Danika Bathory... Her mother. *'he is the dark.'* She had to wonder exactly what she meant by that. But, a different thought was plaguing her now...

CHAPTER TWENTY:

DANE

She sat waiting, the latte in her hand cooling gradually as she stared out the window of the small cafe. *'Ten minutes late...'* she thought. Typical. She heaved a sigh and raised an eyebrow when she saw the mint green Chrysler pull up in front of the cafe.

Dane stepped out, holding his keys by their ring on his index finger as he slammed the door shut and adjusted his sun glasses. Every female head on the block whipped in his direction to admire him head to toe. Frankie just rolled her eyes and waited for him to come in and sit down.

He went to the counter first, asking the young, smitten woman for his 'regular.' She gave him a giggle, twirled her finger in her hair, and turned to prepare his usual order. Quad shot mocha raspberry. Dane always did appreciate caffeine to a fine degree. Frankie smirked, watching the lovestruck blonde make his coffee. He handed her a generous tip, and his card before turning to the table to sit down.

"Is there anything you won't do to get laid, Dane?" Frankie asked in her most sarcastic tone.

He adjusted his blazer and gave her a light grin. "So what's the deal? What's so important that we had to meet up today?" He asked in his usual, carefree tone.

The look on Frankie's face made him pause for a moment. He could see something in her eyes that he hadn't ever seen before. Something had changed her.

"What's going on, Frankie? Talk to me." He took off his glasses as he said it, his eyes, blue as the ocean, peering right into her. She had always found comfort there, in his eyes. They had always somehow made her feel so safe. *He* always made her feel safe.

She swallowed hard, unsure of what she was doing. Unsure if she should even mention it. But, she had to know. "Did you...." She hesitated.

"Spit it out, girl." Dane said with a chuckle.

She just looked at him, her eyes like those of a fawn that had lost it's way. His brow furrowed with worry. "Spit it out..." He said again. Softer this time.

She stared at him for a moment, trying to grip onto the courage to say it out loud. "Did you know I was adopted, Dane?" Somehow, the words came out easier than she expected them to.

Dane sat back in the booth, his weight heaving against the cushions in an unusually thick way. His hands found his face and ran down it in a manner suggesting relief. As did the breath he released in a long, heavy sigh. It was as though he had waited for her to say those exact words for an eternity, and yet hoped she wouldn't. For a moment, he just stared at the ceiling, his hands still lingering at his chin before slapping them to his thighs and sitting forward again, his elbows on the table. "How'd you find out?" He asked quietly.

"Doesn't matter." She said as she spun her cup on the table.

"I guess you're right." He replied, twiddling his thumbs and staring as she spun her cup. It took him a few minutes before he could say what it was he wanted to. "When I was born..." He started, leaning back and slinging an arm over the back of the booth seat. His eyes were still pinned to the table as he spoke. "I tore mom up pretty bad, I guess. After me... She couldn't have kids anymore. She and dad... They always wanted two kids; a boy and a girl. So uh... They decided to adopt." He stopped then, uncertain if he should continue.

She wasn't sure if she should be angry, or sad. She was a bit of both, and didn't know how to express it. "Go on..." She said, choking back a confusing mixture of emotions that bordered on overwhelming. It was true... All of it was true. How was she suppose to feel now?

"Look Frankie, I-" She cut him off then. "Please Dane... Just... Please." She said in earnest.

Dane sighed again, pursing his lips and trying to find the right words. "Mom and dad got a call one day... And, we all went to go pick you up. I was sitting in this chair, listening to the adults talk. I don't even know where we were. It just looked like a church; had all these chairs and crosses all over, ya know." Dane was talking with his hands... It was always a sure sign that he was uncomfortable. Nervous. "Anyway... All I remember from what I overheard, was that they said your mom was..." He hesitated then, and met her eyes. "Tell me." She said softly.

He bit the inside of his cheek and nervously scratched his head. "They said that your mom was in a mental institution... That's all I remember about that day."

Frankie closed her eyes, silently accepting her new truth. It was a confirmation that she needed. All there was to do now, was reopen the folder filled with Danika Bathory's life, and sink deeper into her madness.

She opened her eyes slowly when she felt Dane's hands on her own. "Look Frankie, it doesn't matter who our parents are. It doesn't matter where you or I came from. You're my baby sister. You always have been. You always will be. And, nothing in this world... Not even DNA, will *ever* change that. I'm *always* gonna be your brother. Always." He kissed her hands then and looked at her gently.

She always felt safe there.

CHAPTER TWENTY-ONE:

THERAPY

"The date is March twenty-ninth, 1970. This is Dr. Edwin Haskins. Session two with patient Danika Elizabeth Bathory. Aged twenty-seven years. Caucasian female." Frankie listened intently.

"Danika dear, there is plenty of light now, yes?" He asked gently.

"Yes." Danika's familiar, breathy voice sounded softly.

"How are you feeling today, Danika?" He asked in a chipper sort of tone. There was no reply. He cleared his throat and continued. *"Eh, the maternity nurse has expressed concern to me recently. She says you have been having intercourse, but you won't tell her who you're having intercourse with..."* Frankie's eyebrows shot up at that moment in disbelief of what she had heard. She felt a snicker swell in her chest like a school girl who had just walked in on two teachers bumping uglies.

"Will you tell me, dear?" Haskins asked in a calm, trustworthy tone.

"I already told you his name..." Danika said nervously. Her voice shook in such a way that it seemed she was anticipating something to jump out at her.

"Ah, yes. A Mallard Veephit, if I am not mistaken." He replied, as though reading the name. "It's actually a very clever anagram... I hadn't noticed it until after I had closed my office for the day and I was reading over your file." Haskins' voice was low, and becoming direct as he spoke. Almost as though he was leading her. Trying to make it easier to face her delusion... "Do you know what the anagram is, Danika?"

There was an exceedingly long silence. Just the sound of static over the small speaker. Frankie herself was curious at this point what the anagram was.

"I found it quite fascinating, that you would choose, subconsciously or otherwise, such a man as the sire of your child, Miss Bathory."

Danika's breathing became heavier and more panicked as he spoke. "You don't understand." She breathed.

"I understand that you are having intercourse within the walls of this hospital, Danika. And, there is no way that this man could possibly be the one you're doing it with." He remarked calmly. "Even if this person were not long dead, the fact still remains that you are not allowed visitors. So... This draws the only natural conclusion of either a member of staff, or another patient." He finished.

She stayed silent, save for her rapid, heavy breath. The cadence hinting at a terror that even Frankie could not grasp an understanding of. "We know you're being raped, Danika..." Haskins said gently. "It's not your fault. You're a victim, dear." Frankie felt then like she would be sick. *"But, we have to know who is doing this to you. We can't stop it if we don't know."*

"Mallard Veephit..." She whispered heavily.

"Mallard Veephit does not exist, Danika. It's just an anagram. A figment of your subconscious mind." He was trying desperately to calm her down, and Frankie could tell.

Danika gasped in a breath of air, her voice suddenly becoming steady and eerily calm. *"Perhaps he will come to you in the dark then, doctor. Perhaps he will tear you open like petals of agony and drink from your very being... Maybe he will slither inside of you and take you with merciful violence. Maybe he will love you too... Doctor... And then, we shall call him a figment... Of your subconscious."* As she said it, a small chime echoed over the recorder.

"Unfortunately Danika, that marks the end of our session for this week." Haskins said, seemingly unfazed as he grunted and stood up. *"I want to continue this conversation next week, my dear."* He continued as his voice began to sound further and further away. *"Don't worry... We will get to the bottom of this."* He finished.

Frankie heard a door shut, and the doctor's slow, shuffling steps as he made his way back and sat down once more in his chair. She could hear him breathing unsteadily, and a heavy sigh before he picked up the recorder and spoke. *"The patient has become increasingly withdrawn, and seems locked in the delusion that her rapist is this Mallard Veephit... This eh, of course is an anagram fabricated by her subconscious for the man she believes is the father of her child... Vlad The Impaler."*

CHAPTER TWENTY-TWO:

DARKNESS FINDS A WAY IN

Frankie stared off into nothing, startled in disbelief at what she had heard. It wasn't possible... Was it? She wanted to understand, and yet, could not. Was there more to this puzzle that she was missing?

She jumped at the sound of glass shattering nearby, tearing her uncomfortably from her train of thought. Her fingers gripped hard at the back cushion of her couch as she looked around her small abode, searching for the origin of the sound.

Again, the noise, louder this time. And again, she jumped. It sounded like her stockpile of light bulbs being thrown against the ground in the closet adjacent to her. The thought made her heart skip a beat, and her eyes grew wide in fear and concern. It wasn't a sound like they had fallen. It sounded like they were being hurled from the shelves and smashed on the floor.

She stood slowly, not even pretending she had courage enough to open the door and look inside. Her heart began to race before she even took the first step toward the door. Her palms were sweating uncomfortably, and she was significantly aware of the sound of her breathing. Her eyes darted from the closet door, to her front door, her thoughts in a racing debate on whether or not to check the closet, or leave her apartment.

Another crash, loud enough to wake the dead. She took a step back toward the exit, her eyes so wide, she thought they might come out of her skull. She jumped when the crashing turned suddenly to a sonic banging against the closet door. She gasped out loud, and almost did not recognize the sound as her own. The banging persisted, loud and heavy against the door as though some hulking animal were trying to break free of it.

The wood began to splinter and crack beneath the force of the blows. She had backed away so much that she felt a wall against her, and yet somehow, the closet didn't seem any further from her than it had in the beginning. Her heart was beating ferociously in her ears, and her breath was coming in ragged gasps.

A growling erupted from within the closet that held her frozen in place with terror. The sound seemed to secrete from the very walls around her. A horrific noise like liquid belching from behind the splintering door in incomprehensible threats that shook her to the very core. She wanted to run. But, she was too frightened to even move.

She felt stuck; glued to the wall as the pounding grew louder and louder across the room. With each ear splitting slam, the door would bow and groan, spitting chunks of sharp wood at her. She could see clearly through the crack beneath that the light had gone out inside. Dread choked her as she began to shake.

She fought for a moment to keep control of her composure. *'Run.'* She thought quietly. *'Just run!'* The one place in the world she could feel safe, now no longer held that sense of comfort to her. But, how? How did they get in? She obsessively maintained light in *every* room of her home. It wasn't possible.

A banging at the front door sharply followed those from the closet. She pinched her eyes shut and murmured incoherent prayers to whatever God would listen. Incessant pounding from both sides made her instinctively cover her ears. Hot tears crawled like oil down her face as she slid helplessly down the wall to a huddled lump on the floor. Like a child that saw the monster under her bed, she simply slumped there, hoping against hope that the instance was a dream; that it would somehow go away and she would be alright.

Slivers of wood stuck in her hair, and clung to her shirt. She knew that whatever was there would break through at any moment. The doors simply would not hold that long beneath such powerful blows. She couldn't open her eyes; too frightened to see what was coming for her. A muffled voice, deep and urgent called her name. Over and over, loud and insistent. She smashed her hands painfully against her ears, trying desperately to keep the noise out. She felt herself going near mad. How close was she now to just giving up... Just letting them take her...

With a loud crash, the front door gave. She screamed

out loud and shut her eyes as tightly as she could against whatever was coming in. She couldn't think, and found it difficult to breathe through her panic. When a pair of cold, strong hands wrapped around her wrists like clasps of iron, she felt her panic boil into a primal instinct for survival. She kicked, she clawed, she fought with everything in her against whatever held her so tightly, still refusing to open her eyes. The banging and pounding at the closet still persistently terrifying, she was now being shaken and shouted at.

Mustering every ounce of her courage, she opened her eyes. A rush of immediate comfort fell over her like a warm blanket. Moore, in all his aging, grizzled glory held tight to her wrists, and looked at her in a mixture of worry and fear. He didn't get a word out before the eruption fell once more from the closet.

In a shower of wooden splinters, Moore took stance and drew his gun from the holster at his side, pointing it to the tattered closet door. Frankie, still huddled in a panic against the wall, felt something near relief at the realization that she wasn't the only one now that heard it. But, that relief quickly turned to horror when it struck her... Something really *was* trying to get to her.

Another sonic crash. Moore was steady and unflinching, making Frankie wonder how he hadn't run screaming like a child from her apartment yet. Even *she* wanted to leave. He simply kept his aim and advanced slowly toward the origin of the noise.

"Police!" He asserted. "I don't know who you are, and frankly I don't really give a rat's ass, but you're coming with me!" His lips pursed in discomfort as he inched his way forward. Frankie huddled against the wall watching him, her worry ever growing with each small step he took. "No." She whispered. "Don't open it!"

He glanced over his shoulder to her, cocking an eyebrow and motioning with his empty hand to calm down. As he did, the door exploded outward in a storm of splintering wood and glass with a thunder so loud it could have cracked enamel. In a split second Moore was there, shielding her from the rain of slivers, his thick shirt protecting him. "Jesus ever lovin' Christ!" His voice boomed over the explosion.

The air stilled suddenly, and only small bits of glass from shattered lights sprinkled around them in a glittering fog. It took a moment for their eyes to adjust when they glanced toward the closet and saw the creature thrashing against the light now spilling into it. *They* saw it. It was such a comforting knowledge even through the horror of what was raging before her, lashing out against the light as though the glow were a thousand knives slicing through it. She had to wonder... *How?* It was a question that burned in her.

The monster opened it's cavernous black maw and let out a scream toward them in a fashion more threatening than not. And, at this point, Frankie knew a threat when she heard one. It's black hollows for eyes seemed fixated on her as it shrieked. Lurching backward into the shadows inside, it disappeared as though it had never been.

Though the entire thing lasted only a few seconds, it felt like forever to her. She felt Moore's weight shift and watched silently as he stood. It was like he moved in slow motion. His eyes never left the closet that now stood empty, and in shambles. A mountain of broken glass sat at the bottom, shimmering like ice in the light pouring in from her living room.

Small, shaken whimpers escaped her in light hiccups as she sat there, hugging her knees to her chest. The sound of Moore's footsteps fell in crunching hesitation across the glass and wood on the floor. His arms now looked like he had been in a fight with a feral cat; scratched and lightly bleeding against his pale, leather like skin. He stopped where the closet door was suppose to be, looking all over the tiny, empty room, assessing in his mind what he had just seen. Wondering to himself if what he saw was real. After a few moments he took a half turn and looked at her, his eyes bordering on fear and insanity. "What the bloody Hell *was that?!*"

CHAPTER TWENTY-THREE

MOORE'S CONCERN

The street outside was pleasantly free of more than a handful of people going about their lives in uniform style. Frankie sat staring into nothing as Moore sipped a cup of steaming black coffee; his expression one of deep thought. Usually it was Dane sitting there across from her. Not today.

The cafe wasn't as busy and bustling as it normally would have been. Today there was rain, overcast, and folks forgo their coffee in their rush for shelter during weather like this. Not Frankie. This was her favorite time of year. She loved the rain. Always had. Autumn was heavy with it here. It was her idea of heaven.

Moore's voice sliced through the silence with it's deep uncertainty, ripping her from her thoughts. "We'll talk about whatever that was later..." He began. "Right now, the issue is that I found out you were at the Shady Acres Asylum, and now Danika Bathory is missing." He smeared his thick hands down his face in an exhausted manner; his age beginning to show clearly in his tired features. "Would you care to explain...?" It wasn't so much a question as it was a demand.

Frankie's eyes hadn't left the street outside. She stared at the dance of rain drops that fell to the concrete in an almost mesmerizing fashion. "I needed answers. She had them." She said blandly.

"Where is she, Frankie?" His tone was stern now, near accusing.

She ripped her eyes from the rain and looked at him; her eyes red and puffy from crying. "It took her." She replied. Moore swiped his hand over his balding pate and sat back, heaving out a hard breath. "What took her?"

"You wouldn't believe me if I told you."

He slammed his hand down on the table impatiently, catching himself as he did, and motioning apologetically to her when she jumped. He leaned forward and palmed his face for a moment in exacerbation. "Frankie... At this point, I'm ready to believe anything." He began, his hands doing his talking as well.

She looked at him blankly for a moment, before spilling every detail. His expression never changed as he listened. Her story seemed to take hours to tell, and he simply sat there, quietly soaking in everything she said. When she finished, all he did was sit back and slide his hand over his caterpillar mustache before staring down at his empty cup as though there were something there to see.

"Call me crazy if you want," She started, "I'm telling you the truth." She said it in her most uncaring tone.

"After today Frankie," He said unevenly, "I'd be just as crazy, wouldn't I?"

She looked at him then, wondering if what he'd just

said was an acknowledgment of her truth, or telling her he thought she truly *was* insane.

"Okay, girl." Moore said gruffly, as he motioned for the waitress behind the counter for more coffee. "I need you to listen to *me* now." He told Frankie abruptly.

An ugly thunder roared outside as she sat staring at him. Wondering what it was he wanted to say... Good or bad, she wasn't ready to listen to anything. But, aside from Dane, this man was the only friend she really had.

"I have no idea what the bloody hell that was in your apartment," He began. "But whatever it was, was definitely there. I heard it. I saw that door explode, and there is no earthly reason for it to have happened! Okay? I was *there!*" He said it as though he were trying to convince himself, rather than reassure her. She simply listened, waiting patiently for the point to emerge.

"Your mother..." He took a moment before continuing; rubbing his forehead impatiently as though he couldn't believe what he was about to say. "Your mother was committed by a friend of hers. His name was Eirk... Something. I don't remember his last name right now. But..." He trailed off. She could see his eyes gloss over as his thoughts wandered elsewhere; someplace far in the past.

"She was convinced..." It took him a moment to spit out what it was he had to say. As though he were distracted by the past. "She was convinced she was being raped by the devil... In her mind, the devil was Vlad Tepes." She had heard the same from the taped sessions she listened to. So, she was insane... What was he getting at? "She was convinced that Elizabeth Bathory had made a pact with him. That she would feed him maidens from the castle and town... If he promised her eternal youth and beauty." He worried again at his forehead as the waitress poured him another cup of coffee. He gave her a charming smile, and Frankie had almost felt jealous for a split second. Beneath the stress and bronzed badge, he was a very handsome man, with a very handsome smile. For that brief moment, he was dashing.

"The problem is..." He continued after the coy waitress had sauntered away, "that she promised him her descendants as well." When he finished his sentence, he heaved back into the seat once more, drawing his steaming cup to his mustachioed lips and sipping loudly. "She was pregnant twice in that place." His gruff voice muttered as he clinked the cup back to the table and licked his lips. "Once with Clyde... Once with you." His mind wandered again. He looked confused now; far away and lost. Frankie felt something in the form of pity and dread welling up in her chest like a deep, dark hole. "Everyone thought maybe an orderly... But no one could be sure. She never pointed fingers. She just kept saying 'it was him.' But, she was crazy, right? So, who would believe her...?" His eyes refocused on her, serious and uncertain at the same time. "I'm starting to wonder now, kiddo..." He began in a whisper. "If maybe she wasn't so crazy after all."

Frankie couldn't help but feel that all of this was just a conglomeration of nonsense. But... then again she had felt that way many times now, hadn't she? She pushed the feeling aside; all too aware of what was truly happening to her now.

"Either way," he said, his tone rough and uneven, "That hospital was abandoned years ago. Shut down after a couple of orderlies were caught abusing patients. Rape, violence, drugs, the whole nine. Even the murder of Clyde." He paused for a moment, looking as though he had been taken back in time. "That was the first time I had ever seen a dead body. I was still a rookie for Christ sake. I remember thinking, 'it's not like the movies show.' But... The way we found him..." He looked then like he would vomit. Frankie thanked her lucky stars he didn't. "Danika Bathory disappeared twelve years ago. Her nurse, Abbey, was found in the basement with her throat cut. Sliced clean from ear to ear with her own nail file. There was talk of course, some assumed the orderlies. It was determined later that she had done it herself. But... Nobody has seen hide nor hair of Danika since she went missing over a decade ago." He took another sip, emptying the cup. "Short of her resurfacing, I can't imagine how you'd have spoken to her. Then again, not much about today makes any sense." He never looked up at her when he said it, just stared into the empty mug in his hand.

Frankie looked then out the window, the babble of the street was quiet today. Eerily so. But, it was also beginning to show the first signs of dusk. It was time to get away from the shadows.

CHAPTER TWENTY-FOUR:

A VISIT FROM AN OLD FRIEND

The pair of eyes staring eagerly at her from the tatters of her closet weren't as unsettling as they should have been. In fact, they made her angry. She longed for the simplest of things. And, it infuriated her that these monsters had kept her from experiencing it throughout her life. Peace; a sensation so unknown to her, had eluded her since childhood. And, it was the one thing she needed above all else.

Exhaustion swept over her all at once. Had it really been so bad? So horrific that she hadn't even slept? Evidently so. For she now found herself unable to resist the lure of it's call, and submitted to her desperate slumber.

Bitter cold, and the scent of death, ever familiar came flooding her senses. Something was there. But, what? She slept, and she knew she slept. So, why this feeling? Her answer came all too abruptly as something like ice flitted past her in the dark, too quickly for her to see. She stood alone in the pitch blackness, quivering against the cold and watching her breath escape her lips in puffs of mist. With a frightened determination, she searched the dark, begging her eyes to adjust to the startling lack of light.

She was still in her apartment... Even in a dream. She found a bit of humor in that. Bit by bit she began to see shapes form, familiar but not. Her own and yet not.

A scream from a child shattered the silence around her. Spinning her quick as a top to face the noise. A pair of pale, ivory figures scurried away from her in a macabre dance of twitches and flickers. Like a tape playing in reverse. Heather and Marianne Ingram. The same blue dresses. The same pretty shoes. But, their eyes were a different story. Shriveled empty pits like the center of a rotted apricot. The sight was grotesque. She wanted to scream herself, but somehow could not. They looked like the remains of twin porcelain dolls left over in some ancient attic. Cracked and faded, ugly and worn. Not like the pretty girls they were.

Another whip of ice cold ran past her, spinning her about again. This time what she faced terrified her. All too familiar features twisted in a horrific mask of gray rotting flesh slopping from bone. It fell to the blackness beneath with a sound mocking raw meat slapping the cutting board. The sound matched the smell, both making her wretch inwardly.

Before her, in a smog of black and gray mist, screamed Redimona Pruitt. Her stick like fingers reaching out like decrepit branches on some long dead tree and her gaping mouth emitting the most horrid noise she had heard yet. The screeching wale was like something out of a movie. Warning, foreboding, and angry. Her head jerked and spasmed in such a way that it looked as if it would come off her shoulders. Her howl became louder and louder, forcing Frankie to slam her hands over her ears to somehow muffle the awful noise.

The rictus hand clamped down onto her arm, pulling her closer to the rattling figure of what once was Redimona Pruitt.

"Leave me alone!" Frankie shouted as loud as she could, but her voice could barely tremble. The only response she got was an ear shattering scream from the apparition holding her.

She shot upright in bed, heaving and gasping for air. Sweat poured from her, soaking her sheets. Her eyes darted from one end of her apartment to the other, searching frantically around her for the terror that held her only seconds before. But, there was nothing there. The dream was over.

Even her brightly lit apartment offered little comfort. Her full view of the dark closet brought a sense of fear unmistakable and threatening. Her eyes had some trouble focusing, but she could swear she saw something move. Of course she did, she thought. It was dark... There was always something in the dark. The eyes that peered through the blackness at her seemed familiar now. She had seen them before, though she could not place where, or whom.

A sound like splintering wood came from the depths of the tattered room. Creaking and groaning she saw the rictus hand from her nightmare emerging from the darkness of the closet. It crackled and blistered in the light of her apartment, but it did not flee.

She found herself huddled in the corner clutching her blanket, unable to tear her eyes from the figure emerging from the dark. It was being burned by the light; crackling and smoking... But it did not retreat. The light was destroying it... And, yet it persisted. It reached for her from across the room, desperately it seemed. Like it had to reach her. It had to touch her.

The smell was like something out of a morgue. She tried to hold her breath but her panic would not allow it. The stench was more than she could bear.

With a loud groan the necrotic thing lurched back into the dark, seemingly unable to handle anymore light. She didn't know what to feel. It seemed all she knew anymore was fear. Wretched things reaching for her in the night, crawling from the darkness to drag her in, like Danika... She was almost lost in her thoughts when an explosion tore from the closet, covering her apartment in glass and garment.

CHAPTER TWENTY-FIVE:

THE LETTER

Gazing at the disaster around her, she felt a sense of anger welling up inside her, where before there had been only fear. This was going too far. Should she just give up?

She found herself focused now on her jacket. It hung precariously over a chair amidst the havoc created by her phantom explosion. Peering from the side pocket, was the corner of a familiar envelope. The envelope containing Redimona's letter. Is that what this was about?

She just stared. No matter how many times she tried to convince herself to, she couldn't find the willpower to leave her bed. She simply sat there, staring at that envelope. She had forgotten completely about it. All the chaos subsequent Redimona's death had her mind working on fumes. It felt as though she were battling for her very soul.

It took every ounce of fight in her to fling back her blanket and put her feet on the floor. She could feel the shards of glass beneath them, and flinched at the idea of being cut. She only had to reach a bit before she was able to clasp the exposed corner of the letter between her fingers, and settle back onto the bed.

For a moment, she was undecided on whether she

should dare read it or not. She flipped open the envelope and pulled out the neatly folded parchment. It smelled like sandalwood. One of her favorite scents. Perhaps it was deliberate?

My Dear,

You must forgive my rather abrupt exit of this life. I can sense my death coming like a thief in the night. They come for me. You know too well what I speak of. The black dogs that howl at your door, have now burst through mine and I can no longer sustain them. I write this not to tell you I must go, but to tell you you must fight. There are many things you do not yet understand. But, I can shed some light on some of the missing pieces.

Our great lineage is vast and endless, child. My sister, Danika, was not the first to be afflicted with this. It began with our ancestor, The Countess Bathory. It was she that granted us the sight, and brought the darkness into our lives. A pact with the devil, if you will. The sacrifice she made for her eternal youth and beauty, was us. The women of her line. You my dear, are one of those women. As am I. As is your mother, Danika. We belong to the darkness. To him. Your mother was not as mad as she seemed. The man that took her; the man that gave you life, was indeed all she said he was. But, not a man at all. Not of our world anyway.

The dark is an entity unto itself, child. It is where nightmares are born, and live forever. You must not forget that it has life. But, more than that, you must never forget what it craves. You see, the darkness is just that. Devoid of light and vision. An empty place. The beings that lurk there, are simply mirror images of ourselves. With one exception; they cannot see in the darkness they live in. And that my dear, is what they crave the most. They know our world, and they want inside. So, they haunt us. They want us because they crave life. Light. Most are oblivious to their presence. But, there are those of us with the gift if you will, to know they are there, and where they come from. Those of us who have seen.

Of course, there are times they simply play on the fears of others. Frightening children in the guise of some boogeyman. Even going so far as to take a person or two, or at least their lives. We are but playthings. Puppets, as it were. But, all in all, most of us are blind.

Once they have taken me, they will come for you. It falls on your shoulders now to find a way out. Find a way to keep in the light. I should have told you sooner, and I am sorry to have kept you blind to your fate. But, you can change it. Keep focus on what is most important. There are answers you should not seek. Stay in the light, my dear Niece.

I love you so,

Redi

Somehow she knew it would turn out that way. Nothing in Redimona's letter surprised her. It gave her a bit more insight... But, was it insight that she wanted? She had the majority of her questions answered now. But, it all seemed so ridiculous. Countess Bathory? Her ancestor? Frankie was left not knowing whether to laugh, cry, or rip her hair out in frustration. The darklings were real, she knew that much. She had spent her entire life hiding in the light from them. Redimona said to stay in the light. To find a way out. Like she had all her life? Like Danika had? There had to be more to this life than avoiding shadows. She could not just sit on her bed forever hoping they didn't reach her.

For a moment she stared at the letter in her hands, only to have her gaze lifted in disdain to the closet. This was her life...

This was her life...

CHAPTER TWENTY-SIX:

ABANDONED

She stared in the mirror for what felt like hours, trying to figure out if what she was seeing was real. She would blink, her reflection would not. She would breathe, her reflection would not. Certain subtleties that most take for granted. Things that generally go unnoticed, but today, she noticed.

She swallowed hard, unsure whether she should dismiss it as an over stressed imagination or not. After all, she had seen and heard enough to know that anything is possible. And, Redimona's letter... "They are but mirror images of ourselves." Did she stare now at a reflection of herself? Or was it something else?

She felt lethargic. She didn't even want to move. She simply stood there for a time, wondering at her reflection. It seemed to take every ounce of her strength and willpower to tear her gaze away and step into the shower. *Ignore it*, she thought to herself.

A crash of thunder caught her attention and a sudden sense of dread took over. A storm. Great. Storms often lead to power outages. No power, would leave her in the dark. The sound of the rain beating down on the roof was enough to make the deaf cover their ears.

The shampoo in her hair ran into her eyes, stinging and burning at them. Another boom of thunder above, and even with her eyes pinched shut from the sting, she could see the lights flicker. She hurried to rinse her hair, trying desperately to clean herself up before the lights gave.

The buzzing of the light above her signaled another flicker at least. If not a complete outage. The more she hurried, it seemed the less she got finished. Soap still clung mercilessly to her hair when the bathroom light gave in. She froze, and found her breath catching in her throat. She turned off the water and opened her eyes against the burning, trying to focus.

Something like a vice clamped down on her arm through the shower curtain so hard she thought it would break. A scream loud enough to wake the dead came from the other side. Something inhuman. She fought against whatever held her as though her life depended on it. For all she knew, it probably did. She tore away from the iron grip and slipped in the soapy film on the shower floor. Her head knocked against the wall as she fell, disorienting her slightly.

The light flickered back on and she could see a face molded into the shower curtain. Something twisted and evil, lurching for her. It screamed against the light and vanished as quickly as she had seen it, leaving only the sound of breaking glass behind it.

She sat shaking, trying to collect her bearings. She was terrified. Of course there was a storm... It was the last thing in the world she needed right now.

She made several attempts to stand before she was clear headed enough to actually succeed. When she stepped out of the shower, something sliced through the bottom of her foot with searing pain. Sucking a sharp breath through her teeth, she looked down to see the pieces of her shattered mirror littering the floor. She bent to check her foot, and noticed that her reflection in the pieces didn't do the same. They remained standing, staring at her through black hollow pits where her eyes should be.

The blood falling to the floor from the massive cut seemed to sink into the pieces of the mirror and disappear. As though it was being absorbed or collected. The images began to writhe and twitch, but still stared at her with those empty black sockets as though she knew something she was not aware of.

She ran as quickly as her legs would allow from the bathroom, not even bothering to get a towel. She pulled a rag from her kitchen and sat on her bed only a few feet away, wrapping her foot as tightly as she could, hoping to stop the bleeding. She shuffled through her mass of blankets and books until she found her cell phone, and immediately dialed Dane's number.

"Hello?"

"Dane! Dane I need your help!" She pleaded frantically. "Frankie, what's going on?" Dane seemed annoyed, but she needed him. Even if it was only his voice, she needed him. "Something is happening to me, Dane... Something awful. The dark it's-" He cut her off then, "Frankie, is this about the darklings again?" She was silent for a moment before answering.

"Yes, but I-" Again, he cut her off. "Look kiddo, you've gotta stop this! I'm working, okay? I've got to show a house, and my nuts are in a sling as it is! I'll be there when I'm done working. Okay? I promise." She whimpered quietly to herself. "Dane... I need help. Please. They're here." Dane was quiet. For a moment all she heard was his breathing. "I'll be there after work." Then silence. She closed her eyes and simply let the phone drop.

She felt alone. She was alone. How could Dane just abandon her like this? She considered calling officer Moore, but there was really no point. What could he do? Another blast of thunder outside, and the lights went out. She was alone... And, she was in the dark.

CHAPTER TWENTY SEVEN:

THE WORLD THROUGH MY EYES

She could barely see. Her panic grew with every passing second. This couldn't happen. Terror swept through her in waves as the door to her bathroom creaked open. She was shaking uncontrollably and frozen in fear. She could not even will herself to move. Everything in her was screaming at her to run, but her body just wouldn't move.

Footsteps, wet and heavy came slow and awkward from the bathroom. Even through the dark, what she saw emerging was terrifying. What should have been a woman, or a reflection of herself, was covered in some black muck that dripped thick and stringy from her fingers. Long hair hung over her face, dripping with the same. The narrow body was thin and sunken in, pronouncing bone and gut under the gray, slick flesh.

It turned to face her and she ran for the door. She didn't even care that she was naked anymore. She just needed out. But, where her door should have been, there was nothing. Just blackness. She screamed in frustration and pounded on the wall there, desperate for a way out.

She turned to face the hallway, listening to the wet footsteps as they became closer, louder. She ran for the other side of the room, to the windows. Only to find that same blackness. She screamed again, pounded again. But there were no windows there. She was trapped.

She didn't want to turn to face the horror approaching her, but she had to. *Face your fears*, they said. She knew better than to think this was a hallucination. This was all too real.

The chill of the wall against her back was almost comforting. It meant there was something there. Her foot throbbed and burned under the cloth now. She tried to focus on the pain, hoping that would make all of this go away somehow. If she didn't think about it, maybe it wouldn't be there. Wishful thinking.

With nowhere to run, all she could do was watch. Each sloshing step brought it closer, and it was painfully slow. She could fight; but how would one kill the dark? A million thoughts raced through her head at once, none of them making much sense to her. She felt helpless.

It looked like her. Some skeletal, charred version of her. It's face was sunken in and flesh flaked off the bone, like something out of a nightmare. It smelled like rancid meat and sulfur. It was almost close enough to touch her now. Her panic rose tenfold when it lunged for her.

It's decrepit hands clamped down on either side of her face and began squeezing with an insurmountable strength. No matter how she screamed against it, it's grip got tighter and tighter. The immense pressure was so unbearable that she thought her head might collapse beneath the slick, mucky vice.

She dug her nails into it's shoulder and felt her own shoulder being torn at. She cried out at the pain in time with the monster holding her. It's howl was deafening. Like the cry of some wounded beast. She could feel it's flesh, thick and slimy beneath her fingernails as she swiped at it again.

It's injuries did not bleed, but oozed that same black, tar-like substance that covered it and dripped into sticky puddles that disappeared into the shadows. Those same hollow pits for eyes seemed to be staring right at her. Looking at her like she had something that belonged to it. No matter how she fought it, no matter how it twitched and jerked inhumanly, it seemed to stare right at her.

She swiped at it's face, tearing it's flesh in ragged strips down to it's chin, feeling her own face sting and burn at the same time. She screamed against the pain, as did the creature until it released it's grip on her. She ran immediately toward the bathroom, where she knew there would be broken glass to use as a weapon.

She made it to the door when she was spun about and pushed hard. She felt the glass slice up her back as she landed on top of the shattered mirror scattered on the floor. Dizziness, and a sense of momentary shock set in, and she heard the agonizing howl of the thing that now straddled her and held her down. Her vision blurred and faded, and the more she fought, the more she felt the glass slicing at her back and shoulders. Tears, hot and thick began falling down the sides of her face. She felt her willpower fading, seeming so pointless to fight anymore. But still, she tried. The gaping maw above her screamed it's dismay in a terrifying show of fury. Something like a rippling mass of rotted liquid came pouring from the empty sockets of it's eyes and scurried over it's face, disappearing into it's mouth.

It grabbed a mass of her hair and slammed her head hard against the floor, disorienting her. Her limbs went weak. She couldn't even find the strength to lift them. There was nothing left. Only the sensation of those decrepit hands caressing her face gently now. Almost in awe of her.

An immense pressure, and blinding pain filled her left eye in a white hot flood. She screamed at it and writhed, fighting as hard as she could to get her limbs to work. She could feel blood, thick and hot running down her face. A snap, and then shock.

She watched as the thing lifted it's hand to it's face, working something into it. After a moment, it's hand stopped moving, and slowly pulled away, revealing a single eye. It looked all about, taking in each sight, as though it were a child delighted with a new toy. In that moment, it almost seemed innocent. When it's gaze returned to her, she knew what would happen now. More pressure, more pain. It was too much to bear. Too much to fight anymore. She gave in, and let oblivion take her.

"Oh my God! Frankie!" Dane's voice came muffled and low. "Frankie, what did you do to yourself?!" She could feel arms around her. But, she could not move. She sensed his chin on her shoulder, but she could not hold him. She just hung there, empty and lifeless as he clung to her.

 "Frankie, what did you do?!"

CHAPTER TWENTY EIGHT:

UNDERSTANDING

It was a logical question; *how did she remove the other eye?* In reality, no one could have done it. Shock would have set in from the way she had removed the first one. She wouldn't have been able to do it twice.

A white coat strolled into the waiting area and immediately sought out Dane. "She's alive. Though, we aren't sure how. The surgery went well. She is resting comfortably, and with any luck, she'll pull through."

"Thank you, doctor." Dane said in a hushed tone. "Can we see her?" He finished.

The doctor gave it a moment's thought before responding. "She is not well enough, that will take time, you understand."

"I know doc, but please... I need to see her." Dane was sincere. He seemed so helpless now. Like an abandoned child.

He looked to Dane with true understanding and sympathy, and placed a hand on his shoulder. "Alright, but only for a few minutes. She needs rest."

"Thank you, doc! Thank you." Dane whispered before charging down the hall. Anderson followed close behind. The corridor seemed to go on forever. It felt almost suffocating. The sounds of suffering came from every direction. It felt like ages before they reached the elevator. Two floors up and four corridors later, they reached Frankie's room. What they saw, would change them forever.

From where she lay, an eerie black mist began receding from either side. Like a blanket of shadows parting and melting into the walls. Like it was running from them. A nurse sponged Frankie's arm, seemingly oblivious to what was happening around her. They both simply stood there, jaws agape, unable to believe what they were seeing. They looked at each other and knew, they had both seen the same thing.

"There you go, sweetheart. Nice and clean." The portly nurse said gently as she stroked Frankie's hair. Frankie groaned quietly, and stirred a bit. She was waking up. The nurse left the room, giving them a sweet smile before disappearing around the corner.

Her head above the nose was covered in bandages, as were her torso and shoulders. Dane could see grotesque claw marks running down her pretty face, and knew they would leave scars. Her last words kept repeating themselves in his head, tearing at him. *Please, help me.* And, he refused. This was the result. He left her. Abandoned her. The mist they just saw... Was what she had said all these years true? No. There had to be a logical explanation to what happened.

Dane and Anderson both took a side of her bed and held her hands. She flinched, shooting her head from one side to the other as though she could see them. And, she could. But, what she saw looked like what they would have if they had been buried for ages in some slick pit of tar. She began to twist and fight against their grip on her. "Frankie! Calm down, it's me! It's Dane!" It was his voice, but it couldn't be him. This was not Dane. "Frankie, it's Dr. Anderson. We need you to calm down. It's alright now. You're safe here." The voice was comforting, just as Dane's... But, she did not see them. Only these twisted howling things that held her.

All at once she remembered. That thing... It took her eyes. But, she could see? This place was not the world she knew. It was like every description of hell, minus the light. Devoid of everything but the figures surrounding her. Each horror she had faced before, now amplified a million times. "Frankie..." Dane's voice fell again. She stopped fighting, turning her head from one figure to the other, finally grasping what it was that Redimona had tried to tell her. This world beneath the world. The lifted veil. What lay behind the curtain. They finally had her. Like Danika, and Redimona. They had her.

"Frankie, talk to me, please." She turned her gaze to the befouled image of Dane. He could not help but feel that she was staring right through him. It was an unsettling feeling.

"Stay in the light." She whispered.

Redimona's words rang clear as day as Frankie fell into a hysterical spiral of unfettered laughter.

I am the one with no eyes, yet you are the one who is blind.

CPSIA information can be obtained
at www.ICGtesting.com
Printed in the USA
BVOW03s1058131116
467714BV00001B/24/P